I0563751

Encore

by

Bernadette Marie

5 Prince Publishing, Denver Colorado

This is a fictional work. The names, characters, incidents, places, and locations are solely the concepts and products of the author's imagination or are used to create a fictitious story and should not be construed as real.

5 PRINCE PUBLISHING AND BOOKS, LLC

PO Box 16507
Denver, CO 80216
www.5PrinceBooks.com

ISBN 13: **978-1-63112-019-0** ISBN 10: **1631120190**
Encore
Bernadette Marie
Copyright Bernadette Marie 2013
Published by 5 Prince Publishing
Front Cover Viola Estrella
Author Photo: Damon Kapell

Third Edition/Third Printing February 2014 Printed U.S.A.

5 PRINCE PUBLISHING AND BOOKS, LLC.

For Stan,
who believes in every crazy thing I come up with

Acknowledgements

The journey to getting the Matchmaker series out to my readers has been a long fought one with battles that included blood, sweat, and a lot of tears.

My Fab 5, my husband, and my family, I thank you for being there every step of the way. You were amazing support for me.

Susan Loher, how can I ever thank you enough for being there for me. Thank God for the little miracles in storms!

Connie Kline, you battled for this! You came to the front line! Thank you!

For June, Lynae, Carolyn, and Victoria, a super BIG thanks for being the first set of eyes.

Dear Reader,

Matchmaking is an art and a skill passed down from generation to generation.

Welcome to *Encore*, where Sophia Kendal takes her turn at playing matchmaker for her daughter Carissa, and her dear friend Thomas Samuel. Follow their journey as they learn that you can create your own fates in life and love.

My sincere thanks goes out to those who had the chance to read *Matchmakers*, the first book in the Matchmakers Series before it was published. It was the desire of these women who wanted more matchmaking and Carissa's story that prompted me to write two more books.

I hoe you enjoy Carissa and Thomas's venture into a love neither of them thought they could have or deserve and will join us for the final book, *Finding Hope*.

Happy Reading,
Bernadette Marie

Encore

Chapter One

Her young student pulled the bow across the strings of the violin, and the sound was pure evil. Carissa Kendal winced, then quickly smiled. She'd get it in time. Eventually, they all got it if they stuck around.

The dropout rate of students was the one dark cloud over her next venture, the Kendal School of Music. It had been her dream to teach music in her own school, and she was about to dive into it. She'd hoped her mother would want to be by her side more, but Sophia still had Hope to raise. Carissa had accepted that, but to have her mother call up an old friend to help her wasn't settling.

Did Sophia not think she'd look him up? That she wouldn't find out who he was?

At the moment, he was nobody. Every musical endeavor he'd pursued in the eight years since the renowned tenor Pablo DiAngelo's ensemble broke up had failed spectacularly.

Why was Sophia soft on him? Her mother's name carried far more influence than that of the failed pianist, and it would have given Carissa's music school all the prestige it needed.

The student pulled another evil note and snapped Carissa from her thoughts.

"I'm never going to get this," the young girl complained with her nose wrinkled.

"You will. If you want to, you'll get it." She smiled encouragingly, remembering when she'd been that young girl. "You need to remember to practice the material I give you." Carissa raised her eyebrows with the subtle demand.

"Okay. I promise I'll be better next time."

And if you practice, that will always be the case."

As her student gathered her instrument, Carissa marked off her lesson sheet and handed it to her.

They left the study of the old boardinghouse, where Carissa lived with her grandmother, and stood by the door as her student's mother walked toward them. Carissa gave the girl a squeeze on her shoulder.

"She's doing wonderfully. A little extra practice each day will help," she said. "Don't forget your peppermint on your way out the door."

The young girl fished in the bowl for the right piece of candy as Carissa opened the front door. The violinist's mother handed Carissa a check for the lesson.

"Thank you, Carissa. She enjoys her lessons very much."

"I'm pleased to hear that. We'll see you both next week."

As the woman and her daughter descended the front steps, a man paid a cab on the street in front of the old house. He stood with his suitcase in his hand and looked her way.

He was tall and too thin for her taste, but he looked almost regal in the way he carried himself. He removed his sunglasses and stroked the wisps of dirty blond hair from his eyes. She almost didn't recognize the man from the pictures she'd seen on the Internet.

He looked like a blond Jimmy Stewart, and her stomach did a little flip.

"Hello," he called as he neared the house. She smiled despite her misgivings. He even walked like Jimmy Stewart.

Like most of Pablo's ensemble, he'd always walked behind the man with the million-dollar smile, never next to or in front of him, not like her mother who had been paraded on Pablo's arm. It was no wonder she hadn't recognized him.

She extended her hand to him, and as his fingers enclosed hers, she gulped in air. He was strikingly handsome. She hadn't expected that.

To have played for Pablo, as Sophia had, Thomas had to be tremendously talented. Yet would the curse that hung over his career affect her music school?

"You must be Thomas Samuel. I'm Sophia's daughter, Carissa Kendal. I've heard a lot about you."

When Sophia Kendal had said her daughter would meet him at the boardinghouse in Kansas City, he hadn't expected she'd look like the woman standing before him. The woman before him stood erect as a dancer. Her hair fell to the middle of her back like an ebony waterfall, and her dark eyes were soft. She wore a flowing, orange blouse and a long skirt of the same orange, mixed with earthy browns that swirled around her calves when she moved.

She was mesmerizing.

"Please come in." She stepped back through the door. Heat rose on the back of his neck as he passed by her. "My mother says you'll be staying with us until you get settled."

"Uh. Yes." He felt like his tongue had swollen. "I'm sorry if I seem out of sorts. I knew Sophia for so long that to think of her as your mother, well, that's a stretch for me."

Carissa smiled at him again. "I was seventeen before she adopted me, so I can understand. I'm sorry you couldn't make it out for their wedding."

"Yes, so am I." Had he made that wedding, he'd have made it his business to become more familiar with the dark beauty who, with the most subtle gesture of tucking her hair behind her ear, had his pulse climbing.

Guilt halted his thoughts. He should have been at the wedding because he'd promised Sophia he would be. It was just another broken promise, and he feared he would let her down again. And given his past, he had no business fantasizing about Carissa—or any woman. It could end only in heartache—or worse.

"So you're a teacher?"

"Yes. That's my dream, to bring music to the masses through their own fingers."

"You play the cello, right? Just like your mother?" He asked nervously.

"Yes. Even before I met her, she was my inspiration."

"Why are you only giving lessons? Why aren't you in the symphony?" From what he knew, Carissa's talent was as superior as her mother's.

"I'm a caregiver. My mother needed to look after my little sister, and I chose to take care of the women who took care of me growing up." Her dark eyes clouded with sadness. "My aunt Millie had cancer, and we lost her about six years ago."

"I'm so sorry." He fought the urge to reach out to her.

"Thank you. Now I'm taking care of my grandmother, who will be ninety-two soon."

"She lives here? With you?"

Carissa nodded. "Well, I live with her. But yes, and she's still feisty as ever."

"I heard that," an elderly woman called as she walked from the kitchen, slowly, balancing with a walker.

"Katie," Carissa said, "this is Mr. Samuel. The man mom sent over."

"Mr. Samuel, it's nice to meet you." He shook her hand with a gentle grasp. "Thank you. And please call me Thomas."

"All right, I will." She turned to Carissa. "I'm going to go lie down. Get Thomas settled. I think your parents will be over soon for dinner. Wake me when they arrive."

Thomas's belly clutched. Sophia and David were coming for dinner. Suddenly he felt dizzy. He hadn't sat down to a meal with a family in a very long time. It shouldn't bother him; this was Sophia, after all. He'd spent plenty of time with Sophia.

What would she think of him now? Now that he was washed up, broke, and had failed at everything he had always hoped he'd accomplish.

Carissa kissed her grandmother on the cheek. Thomas watched the exchange. He'd known them both but moments, yet he knew what they meant to each other. He was envious.

"Thank you again, Mrs. Burkhalter, for letting me stay here with you."

"You can stay as long as you call me Katie." She gave him a stern nod.

"Yes, ma'am, Katie."

Katie made her way down the hall to a bedroom and shut the door behind her.

"Wow." He shook his head. "I feel like I've just met a legend. For years I heard about Sophia's grandmother. I feel like I've known her forever."

"Next to my mother, she's one of the most amazing women to me." Carissa's eyes followed the path her grandmother had walked, her devotion to the older woman glistening in her expression. "Why don't I show you to your room, and you can get some rest before dinner." She turned back to him, catching his stare. "I'm sure it was a long flight from Rome."

"Yes, it was." Too long. Every minute of the flight he'd fought with himself over whether it'd been right to accept Sophia's job offer. He followed Carissa up the stairs.

The room was as large as his apartment in Rome, yet more homey. It had a brass bed that looked as old as the house. Two chairs sat on either side of the window with a marble-topped table between them. A door stood ajar, revealing an adjoining bathroom, so he wouldn't need to share facilities with others in the house.

The room felt masculine, and that pleased him. He'd been worried about staying in the house of an old woman, with doilies under everything and untouchable collectables, and had almost called a hotel and made reservations. He was glad he hadn't.

"This room was my father's while we lived here. I think you should find it suiting." Carissa pushed back the sheers, and the afternoon light filled the room.

"I think this will be wonderful."

"Good." She pushed open the bathroom door. "Your bathroom is through here. It adjoins to the other room, but no one uses that room anymore."

"Anymore?"

She let out a laugh that was as mesmerizing as her looks. "That was my room, on the other side. When I moved back in to take care of my grandmother and aunt, I took my mother's old room. It was her room growing up. It's really big and has its own bathroom." The smile that danced on her face was childlike. "So if you need anything, I'm just down the hall."

Her innocent offer punched him in the gut. He only nodded as he watched her leave. He already knew he'd be in need of her. And because he couldn't allow himself to have her, his nights here would be miserable.

He forced himself to focus on Sophia's school. An entire school dedicated to bringing music to children. Too many school districts had ripped it out of schools because of funding. The idea was stellar! Her request for his help in putting it together had sent his dragging self-esteem through the roof. It hadn't taken but a week to pack his few belongings and board the one-way flight to America to start a new chapter in his life, right there in Kansas City, Missouri.

He had learned so much from Sophia when he'd started playing with Pablo. To work with her on something as great as a school made his heart pound.

There was a snag, of course. Carissa Kendal would assuredly be one of the teachers.

He squeezed his eyes shut and pushed away the thought. He wasn't looking for a woman. He wasn't looking for the complications of a relationship. He didn't come from the kind of family that embraced love and commitment. That, he knew, had to run deep enough to run through one's blood. Thomas Samuel was an amazing musician and composer—but lover, husband, or father material? He'd never know. He'd never bring a woman into his circle and hurt her like that. Because that's what he'd do. He'd hurt her, just as his father had hurt the ones he was supposed to love.

He blew out a breath. They had a lot in common, the members of Pablo's ensemble. Pablo had run from whom he was. Sophia had run from what she thought. Thomas had run from what he might become.

He'd run for a long time. He'd left the States when he was only seventeen and started touring with Pablo almost immediately. He'd been Pablo's prodigy. Far away from his family, if you could call it that.

His family didn't live too far from where he currently stood questioning his very being. Fear fluttered in his heart. Occasionally he let himself dream of being part of a family again, but he knew it could never come true.

As it was, he was going to wash up, go downstairs, and dine with Sophia's family. A family he already knew a great deal about. But the nerves wouldn't subside. They were a family and he was an outsider, just as he'd always been. A commotion filtered through the house, and Thomas followed the sound toward the wonderfully large kitchen. With her back turned to him, Carissa stood at the sink beside her mother. Heat rushed through him.

They were laughing, joking, and bumping into each other over the sink.

"If you'd move your big behind..." Sophia directed the insult to Carissa.

"Oh, excuse me, Miss-I-Haven't-Seen-a-Treadmill-in-a-Year," Carissa boosted back, and they both laughed.

He could see that happiness had landed on Sophia. She'd always been a firm and taut person, but the few pounds that had crept onto her let him know she was truly joyous in her role of wife and mother.

"Who are you?" a small voice asked from the table.

The laughter died, and Thomas turned his head to the table where Katie sat. A young girl with rosy cheeks, deep blue eyes, and mounds of blonde curls sat next to Katie, looking up at him. He smiled cautiously at her.

"I'm Thomas. Who are you?"

"I'm Hope. I'm eight." Her expression clearly said, you should have known that.

"Thomas!" Sophia squealed as she grabbed for a towel to wipe her hands on, and then she raced across the room and wrapped her arms around him.

He breathed her in.

She pulled him back at arm's length to study him, and he did the same. Her auburn hair was a bit longer, but her brown eyes were just as welcoming. When she smiled at him, he knew he'd found a home. One thing about Sophia, she could always make him feel at home.

"I can't believe you're here. I can't believe you're standing right here." Tears formed in her eyes, and she pulled him to her again. He held her tight. Already, he was glad he'd come.

"How come there is some man hugging my wife in the kitchen, and you are all standing around watching?" Thomas stiffened at the sound of the man's voice.

"Daddy!" Hope ran into the man's arms and embraced him. Still in his pilot's uniform, he bent down to hug his daughter. "This is Thomas. He knows Mommy."

"Well, maybe you should introduce us."

Hope nodded and walked her father by the hand to Thomas, who still held one arm around Sophia.

"Daddy, this is Thomas."

"Thomas, it's nice to meet you. I'm David Kendal." He extended his hand, and Thomas shook it.

"It's an honor to meet you. I feel like I know you very well."

"Considering the time frame in which you got your stories, I'd beg for another chance to make a first impression." He touched his wife's cheek, and she moved forward and kissed him gently.

"Mr. Kendal, she never had a bad word to say about you." He looked at Sophia.

"She should have come home sooner then."

Sophia threw up her hands and shook her head with a smile. "You know, I'm not going to stand here and relive the fact I made a mistake years ago. Is there anyone in this kitchen who doesn't think I'm a wonderful granddaughter, mother, friend, and wife?"

They shook their heads.

"Okay then, everything ended well, and we can eat."

Thomas found himself seated between Hope and Carissa at the dinner table. If he let himself look at Carissa, he was sure he'd end up tripping over his tongue like a lovesick puppy, so he made an effort to take an interest in her younger sister. One look at Hope and he saw similarities to Carissa, though Hope was fair and Carissa's complexion darker. The resemblance was amazing for an adopted child.

Katie passed the salad bowl over the top of Hope, who wrinkled her nose. With a nod from Katie, Thomas dropped a small spoonful onto her plate, and Katie smiled. She reminded him a little of his own grandmother.

"So, Thomas, you're a pianist?"

"Yes, ma'am. I've been playing piano since I was three."

"That's awfully young."

"Well, my grandmother insisted, and she taught me my very first scales." The memory was one of the few from his childhood that could bring a smile to his face.

"Wise woman."

David passed a plate of roast to Katie. "So, are you sure you're up to helping these two with their school? They can be awfully demanding."

"I can't tell you how excited I was to get Sophia's call. What's happening with music programs in schools is pitiful. It doesn't make sense to take the arts away. When you start doing that..." All eyes were on him, and he realized he was about to go on a rant. "Well, I think it's foolish, and bringing music to others is what I do best."

He felt Carissa's eyes on him, and he turned to catch her stare. Her cheeks flushed immediately, and then she turned away. He sucked in a breath and lifted his water glass to his lips to try to cool off his racing mind.

Carissa dipped her head toward her plate and buttered her roll. He believed in the cause. Yes, that was what she'd hoped for. She wasn't sure he was going understand the mission. After all, he was a down-and-out performer, and she was a teacher.

She'd been so conflicted with her mother's idea of bringing Thomas into their school. And now that he was here, all she could think about was him, not as a musician or teacher, but as a man. A man whose passion for sharing the gift of music she found more than attractive.

She took a bite of her roast. Did Thomas feel the heat between them, or was that just her?

His hypnotic blue eyes and that disheveled sandy hair that he kept running his fingers through had her heart fluttering. Heat prickled her skin, and that mortified her. She'd felt like this before, just not over someone she'd barely met. And she'd been burned before. This time she wasn't going to jump straight into bed with a guy just because he was hot.

"Don't you think so, Carissa?" her father asked, and she darted her head up.

"I'm sorry, what?"

"Don't you think that school will be operational by the time the schools return from their winter break?" he repeated.

"Oh, yes." She blew out a small breath. "We took possession of the building two days ago. There is a lot of work to be done, and that should take us through December." Thomas's eyes were on her, and she took the courage to look at him and finish, calmly and professionally—the way their relationship would be. "We'll start enrollment in the first part of December. We've talked to the local schools about passing out our information and doing some assemblies for the students. I think we should be able to reach a lot of kids."

"You've already done a lot of work to ensure your success." He shifted his eyes to her mother. "Sophia, I'm so impressed."

"Well, I'm just the silent partner. This was really all Carissa's doing. This is her dream." Carissa smiled as her mother laid a gentle hand on hers.

She leveled her eyes with Thomas's as he turned back to her. That intoxicating blue peered into her soul, and she felt her heart hitch. Against her will, the corners of her mouth turned up into a smile. He grinned at her, melting her resolve.

"Thank you for considering me for your staff. It is going to be an honor to work with you."

That was it. Her heart was gone.

All she had to do was keep Thomas from finding out.

Chapter Two

Carissa gathered dishes while Thomas sat on the back porch with David after dinner. Katie excused herself to bed for the night, and Hope wandered between helping Carissa clean up and diverting her father's attention.

Sophia set the dishes by the sink.

"So, what do you think of Thomas?"

"He seems nice enough, and if you say he's talented, then he should be a wonderful asset to our school." Carissa flipped her hair over her shoulder and turned on the water to fill the sink. She didn't want to tell her mother what she was really thinking of Thomas.

"I think we should all sit down on Sunday during dinner and start addressing some issues about curriculum and what we want to accomplish."

Carissa snapped her head up and shifted her glance toward Sophia. She was loosely throwing around the words "our" and "we" when it came to the school, but it was, in fact, her school, and she had a clear plan on what she wanted to accomplish.

Sophia touched her hand, and Carissa knew her thoughts had been transparent.

"I know you and I have ideas, but we should consider what he has to say. He did come all the way back to the States for this." And that was only one of her problems with Thomas Samuel. First, it was his failed career and his eagerness to leave Rome for Kansas City. Then her body's reaction to him had her practical thoughts dissolving. Now Sophia thought he should have a say in her school when she thought he was just there to teach.

Carissa kept her misgivings to herself and nodded as she looked out the window to the back porch. The October sky had already turned dark, but the porch light illuminated the men like a spotlight.

She watched the interaction between the men and her sister. Hope had landed on Thomas's knee and was showing him something. She couldn't make it out, but he was giving her the attention she was demanding.

Sophia handed her a plate. "Are you sure you're comfortable with him staying here? If you're not, we can find somewhere for him to stay."

"Mom, we'll be fine. If you trust him, I have no reason not to."

"I do."

"I know that. If you didn't, you wouldn't have asked him to be part of the school or stay here with us."

"I think it'll be good to have him here. It's one more set of eyes on Katie." Carissa turned to take the plate from her mother, but Sophia gripped it tightly as though she were afraid to let it go. "I'm worried about her." She shifted her eyes to Carissa.

"I take care of her."

"I know you do. But she's getting frail, and after we lost Millie, I really worried about you."

Carissa began an assault on the dish in her hand, scrubbing it hard enough she could have easily scrubbed a hole through it. "I'll be okay. I know Katie isn't going to be around forever. I just wasn't ready for Millie to go. So, if you're worried that I'm too attached, I'll cope. But she's not going anywhere soon." Carissa shifted her moist eyes to her mother.

"If you're all comfortable that will be good. We can't pay him much. The least we can do is give him a place to live."

Carissa nodded. A place for him to live—where he was only a few feet from where she'd be dreaming about him all night. She steeled herself against letting that thought go any further.

Sophia grinned at her. "And you know, he's single."

Carissa walked her parents to the door. Her father turned to kiss her good-bye and gave her arm a gentle squeeze.

"Call if you need anything."

"I'll be fine. But I promise."

"He's paranoid," her mother said as she kissed her.

Hope ran past them and down the front steps to the car.

"Don't forget. You promised me a juice, too," she called back.

"How could I forget?" Carissa laughed as she waved from the porch.

Sadness washed over her as they drove away. As always, she hated to see people she loved go, even for the night. She turned to go back inside and ran right into Thomas, who was standing behind her. His arms came up. He grabbed her with his hands on her hips, holding her until she regained her balance, then slid his palms up a few inches till his fingers brushed her ribs.

"I didn't know you were standing there." Her voice shook as her hands lingered on his shoulders and his on her waist. The lean musculature, separated from her skin by a thin layer of fabric, drew a soft gasp from her.

"Obviously." He smiled, and her knees went weak. She'd hold on to him a moment until she felt more stable, but not a second longer.

"I guess I'll call it a night." Her eyes locked into his. The porch light shimmered in them, making the warm flecks of gold sparkle within his blue irises. "I want to get to the school tomorrow and start cleaning it out before contractors start working. The last tenants left behind a lot of trash. I need to get a jump on it because I have students on Saturday morning."

Thomas nodded, his hands still sending tingles across her skin. "Saturday morning? I'll need coffee before that first piercing note, but I could help you get started on the cleaning, if you'd like my help."

She smiled and took the necessary step back so he'd release her, though distance between them wasn't what she wanted at all.

"That would be wonderful. Would you mind if we start out about eight thirty?"

"I'll be ready, with my cleaning clothes on."

"Great. I'll repay you Saturday morning with coffee before that first squeaky note. I know a little diner." Her voice was airy and husky, and she realized a bit too seductive for someone she'd just met, but she kept talking, not wanting to leave his presence yet.

"Can't pass that up." He pulled back his hands, raked his fingers through his hair, and her eyes followed his long fingers from his hair until he tucked them into his pockets. "What time do I need to be up for that?"

"That depends. Do you run?"

"Run?"

She nodded with a smile. "Yes, do you run?"

"I should have understood the question better. After all, you are Sophia's daughter." She smiled as he shook his head, and his perfect lips curled into a smirk. "Does she still run all over the damn place?"

"Not so much anymore. She hurt her knee a few years ago. But Saturday mornings, I take a nice run before that first squeaky note." It was that first squeaky note, she thought, that made everything she'd ever dreamed of worth the effort. Her school would be full of squeaky notes, and they would progress into beautiful music someday. She settled at glance at the man who shared her passion for music. Would they too work through their squeaky notes and make beautiful music together?

"Okay then. A run and the promise of good food, good coffee, and good company on Saturday in return for a Friday full of cleaning." His acceptance of her offer snapped her back from her impromptu daydream. "I have a pair of running shoes that haven't been used for running in a long time," he said.

"It's a date then."

"It's a date." He backed up to the door and held open the screen for her as she sauntered through.

Thomas paced the floor in his room. He hadn't returned to the States to find a woman, but one had landed, literally, right on his doorstep, or at least he on hers. And she was his friend's daughter. He hissed out a breath. It was going to take control he'd never had before to keep his hands off Carissa Kendal.

He sat on the edge of the bed, interlaced his fingers together, and tapped his hands against his head. No matter what he did, the image of her wouldn't fade, and the desire for her only grew. It wasn't going to be any use to fight it. He'd met her less than twelve hours earlier, and never in his life had he felt what he was feeling at that moment. When Carissa looked at him, his skin was set into flames, his stomach did flips, and he knew his heart rate had never been so fast. He'd have kissed her right on that front porch, if he were someone else.

Thomas rubbed his hands on his pants. He wasn't someone else. He had to think about his music and his mission. He wasn't here to seduce the daughter of his dear friend. No, he was here to share music with others. That he knew he could do. The question was could he do it with Carissa next to him, making him realize that he longed for those things he'd refused himself. A career. A family. A woman to love.

Carissa pulled out of the driveway Friday morning feeling physically drained. Her night had been restless because she was too aware of the man in the room down the hall. And there was no doubt, when she'd handed him his cup of coffee in the kitchen that morning, that he'd lost some sleep, too. He'd all but jumped and dropped the mug when she'd touched his hand with hers. How could a man as handsome as Thomas Samuel be so skittish around women?

His too-long, blond hair kept falling over his eyes, and he'd brush it over the rim of his sunglasses.

"Why exactly are you cleaning the building before construction? Doesn't construction make a mess?"

She laughed. "Yes, but the previous owners left a bigger one. You'll see when we get there. We can't do construction until the junk is gone."

He nodded and shifted in his seat. "So, when do contractors start?"

"Tomorrow afternoon."

"So this has to be finished today."

"At least the bulk of it. We've done some. The electrician is the only one coming in tomorrow. Then when the plumbing is done, Dad can start on framing the walls."

"Your dad is building the walls?" His voice carried an element of surprise, and she couldn't help but smile. Just one look at Thomas Samuel and one would assume he wasn't the handyman type of guy. Of course, when she'd seen him come into the kitchen that morning, she knew he wasn't the kind of man to do manual labor. He'd worn a pressed white T-shirt tucked into his dark, pristine jeans.

"My dad's no carpenter. The fine trim work will have to be contracted, but he can build a wall," she said with love and admiration for her father.

"When your mother called and asked me to come help, I was under the impression that she was opening the school. I didn't realize she was just helping you." He shook his head and let out a slight grunt of a laugh.

Carissa tightened her grip on the steering wheel. Would he have come if he'd known, she wondered.

Her jaw tightened. She'd thought Sophia was going to be a bit more of a partner in the school too, but instead she'd called someone else in. Carissa wasn't yet sure if she should be hurt or grateful. She slid a glance toward Thomas. For the moment, she'd give him the benefit and be grateful.

"She'll always be my partner. Everyone needs someone to turn to."

"What will she do at the school?"

She gave it a moment's thought and shifted in her seat. "She'll be everywhere for a while. She has a lot of contacts in the community, and we're hoping to draw off that for enrollment. As for being active in the school, I don't think she'll be able to help herself, and she'll be teaching more than she thinks she will. One of the things I want to offer is a music class for homeschooled students. She'd be able to teach in the daytime when Hope is in school."

Thomas slapped his hands on his thighs and let out a gasp of excitement.

"What a great idea! Homeschooled kids whose parents can't teach them music. That's fantastic."

His enthusiasm over her plan made her smile. It's just what she'd wanted. Someone else who believed in her cause, believed in what she could do for the community. Perhaps her mother was right, and he'd have some good ideas.

"Well, someday down the road I'd like to have a band, an orchestra, and even a choir just for homeschooled students. There are more and more of them every year. I, alone, teach seven homeschooled children."

"You teach out of your house?"

"I learned to perfect my skill in that study, and so did my mother. It seemed like the right place to teach others. During the summer, I teach during the day, but during the school year, I teach in the afternoons."

"What do you do when you're not teaching?"

"I practice. You never know when you'll get the one golden opportunity to perform at some venue that would take your breath away."

"Yeah, I understand that." His voice trailed, and she heard the disappointment in it.

"The Vatican?"

"It would have topped them all." He sighed. "It just wasn't meant to be."

Carissa remembered Sophia's quest for the Vatican. She'd left Carissa and her dad to pursue the dream of the ultimate venue. Sophia's dream-come-true moment had almost cost Carissa her own dream of having the perfect family.

Guilt rose in her. She'd been happy when Pablo DiAngelo had ruined Sophia's chance at performing the Vatican. It had sent Sophia back to them, so they could be a family. She'd never given thought, however, that it may have ruined the careers of others—like Thomas.

"Well, this is it." Carissa eased the car into the parking space in front of the old building. The building was like a child looking for a home. It needed to be nurtured and groomed. She'd do just that. With brooms and dustpans, walls and floors, and paint and trim. She'd give it a life, and in return, it would welcome others inside and they would make it their home, just as David had done for her so many years ago. "It doesn't look like much, but it will soon."

"What was this?"

"I think it was a pharmacy." She climbed from the car. "I really never paid attention to it then."

She unlocked the front door and pushed it open. It was like opening the door to a magical world. She walked in. The slightest sound from her sneakers on the floor echoed through the building.

"Isn't it wonderful?"

The lighting was bad. The linoleum tiles on the floor were coming up, and what paint remained on the walls was peeling. It was one, big, open space with an office and a bathroom in the back, but all Carissa saw were endless possibilities.

Thomas stood to her side and swept a look around. He saw nothing but heaps of debris in a building that should be torn down and a better one built in its place. How did she think that in a few months she could turn the dilapidated structure into a music school and make money at it?

He let out a slow, steady, quiet breath. That wasn't him thinking, it was his father, and it killed him that someone else's joy could inspire such negativity in him. He turned back to Carissa, who was still gazing around the space as though she could see everything in its place. "What do you envision?"

"This will be a waiting room for the parents and a reception area. So we'll put a wall here." She raised her hands to help him visualize. "Then through the door…" she said as she boxed it in with her hands as she walked through, stepping over an old rolled-up rug, "there will be two classrooms on either side of the hallway. They'll be private lesson rooms. Then…" Her eyes grew wide as she walked toward the back of the building. She skirted around a set of old display cases with broken shelves. "This area will be open space. We'll do group lessons, orchestra, and band practice here."

She settled her eyes on him, and he worked up a smile.

"Do you have a classroom that could be used for theory classes? Something with space where there could be a chalkboard and desks?"

"Well, that sounds like a public school, not a music school." She laughed when she said it, and he couldn't believe that an actual class of theory wasn't important to her. She was still dancing circles around the room, taking it in. He'd talk to her about it later. But you couldn't have a school without theory as a basic class.

Carissa spun back toward him. "What do you think?" Her hair was pulled back from her face, and it gave him full view of the wonder in her eyes. No matter what he thought of the dingy building with its peeling paint, he couldn't help but get caught up in Carissa's excitement.

"I think I'm honored to be here. The smile on your face is priceless."

Her brows creased. "I guess we should get to cleaning, huh?"

"I think that would be a good idea." Relief washed over him. He needed to be busy because standing there looking at her, in her pair of battered jeans, which hugged her narrow hips, and the plaid button-up shirt, which covered a red tank top and was left open, was enough to raise the heat of his body. Cleaning would be a good deterrent from the thoughts he was having about the collapse of the building—and the things he'd like to do to Carissa.

Carissa shook her arms to get the feeling back in them, then rolled her shoulders to work out the kinks that were forming in her back. She'd been wiping the soap off the front windows for the better part of an hour while Thomas hauled old pieces of scrap wood and shelving to the dumpster.

"This will be a good venture." Thomas walked toward her. "Open your hand."

Just as he'd asked, she held open her hand to him. Gently, he laid a fifty-cent piece on her palm. When she shifted her gaze from the dull coin up to his eyes, warmth flooded through her.

He took her hand and curled her fingers around the coin. "Just think, that's worth fifty lucky pennies." He winked, then turned back to finish his trash duty.

Carissa let her heart settle before opening her hand and looking at the coin. She couldn't help but think he was right. It was a good venture.

They swept, dusted, and mopped. By one o'clock, they had the majority of the cleaning done.

Thomas blew out a breath and wiped the back of his hand over his brow. He pushed the hair from his eyes—those blue eyes that could pierce her in a way no one else's ever had. His perfectly pressed T-shirt had worked its way out of his pants, and there was a streak of dirt on his cheek.

"You have a little something there." She raised her hand to his cheek to wipe it off, but his hand was quicker.

He'd winced. She noticed it as he caught her hand. After a settling moment, he let her brush away the dirt.

"Thank you." His voice cracked.

"My pleasure." She smiled because it was. Carissa's mouth had gone dry from being so close to him. She backed away from him and moistened her lips. "I could use a hamburger. What about you?"

"Shouldn't we go home and shower?"

She swallowed hard as she pushed away the mental image of Thomas in the shower...with her. Her neck heated, and she averted her gaze to the window until she caught her breath. The sky was blue.

"This place is outdoor seating, and it's still nice enough out. What do ya say?"

He tucked his shirt back into the waist of his jeans.

"Okay, but my treat if you're buying breakfast tomorrow."

"You're on." She grinned, hoping her true feelings weren't plastered all over her face for him to see. "And then we'll go get Hope and take her for that juice I promised her. Maybe we could discuss the remodeling plans," she added, hoping to focus her mind back on her work and away from the thoughts about working on Thomas.

He'd laughed when she'd ordered a quarter-pound hamburger with extra ketchup, a large size onion rings, and a chocolate shake.

He wasn't sure he'd ever seen a woman order that much food. His mother never would have ordered anything other than a child-sized hamburger, if they'd ever eaten out, that is.

"Got some appetite." They set their trays down on the table.

"Yeah, well, you were buying. Wanted to get your money's worth."

He wondered where she'd put it all. Obviously, she didn't eat like that all the time. Her body was so perfect. Every curve was in the right place, but it was taut and tight in all the right places, too.

Moving his eyes from her was becoming harder to do—even as she dragged an onion ring through a mound of ketchup and bit it in two. The delight in her eyes from the simple act of enjoying a meal was something he'd never seen in a woman. His mother spent mealtimes catering to her children and her overbearing husband. The women with whom he'd toured in Rome were too worried about their appearance to find pleasure in the fine art of a simple meal.

None of that seemed to matter to Carissa.

A few wayward strands of hair had fallen from the ponytail at the back of her head, and there was a smudge on her forehead. Carissa lived in the moment and reveled in each minute she took in. Watching her lifted his spirits. The desire to feel that passion with his very own hands was overwhelming. He diverted his eyes and focused on a long sip of his soda.

Carissa bit into her hamburger and ketchup spurted from its side and landed on her chin. Laughing, she set down the burger and wiped off her face.

"So tell me, Thomas Samuel, where did you call home before you traveled the world?"

He choked on the soda. He coughed, cleared his throat, and set down the cup. Trying to keep his voice steady, he answered, "Um, I lived in Chicago."

"Chicago?" The word purred from her throat, but still left him with a bitter taste. "Oh, I'd love to go to Chicago someday."

"You've never been?"

"No. I really haven't been anywhere but here." Her eyes glossed with tears.

"You don't like to travel?"

Carissa shrugged. "I never really wanted to be anywhere but here. Here I was safe and taken care of."

It was a vulnerable moment, and his heart urged to ask questions.

He didn't.

He'd like to have known what she meant, but if he asked, then so would she. It was better to leave some rocks unturned.

"What time does Hope get out of school?" he asked instead.

"She gets out at two-thirty. We'll head over to my parents' house to pick her up."

He looked down at the dust on his shirt and then back up at her with a flick of his head to move the hair from his eyes.

"Do we have time to swing by home and get a shower?"

"You are worse than a woman." Her laughter was like a crescendo in a musical movement that dictated his life. He waited for the pause, for the beat to change, but with Carissa, it didn't.

"That's what happens when you live around a man like Pablo DiAngelo for most of your life. He wears off. Trust me, until he demanded I constantly be so perfect, I wasn't."

He'd once thought that being Pablo DiAngelo's prodigy was the path to a new and better life. It had only been a detour, he now realized.

His life had been orchestrated like a fine movement, in tune with everyone else's lives and personalities. He'd thought he was happy, but perhaps it was only contentment. Pure happiness was what he saw in Carissa's eyes when she was with her family, when she spoke of her school, and when she ate a hamburger with too much ketchup.

Carissa shot him a glance and a smile that knocked his heart rate up. He wanted what she had, that zest for life. Even more than that, he wanted her.

They sat in the quaint juice shop where Carissa had worked as a teenager. Thomas sipped on a drink that Hope promised him he'd love and listened as she rambled on about her day in third grade.

He wondered if the little person in front of him would take a breath before delving into another tale, but she just kept going.

"Sylvia Parker is going to invite me to her sleepover. She just got a new dog, and I want one, too."

"I don't see that happening." Carissa shook her head. "Mom isn't much of a dog person."

"Well, I think I could ask." Finally, Hope sipped on her juice.

Carissa smoothed Hope's hair with her hand. "We should probably get you back home to finish your homework."

Hope protested with a grunt. "It's Friday. I'm not doing spelling words on Friday."

Thomas winced. He'd uttered those same words once. Homework had never been his favorite thing to do. Hadn't he learned the hard way to make sure it was done early each night? He watched Hope sip on her drink. There were better ways to teach a child to have responsibility than how he had learned.

"Just think, if you do your homework on Friday, then you have all weekend to play," Carissa said.

"Fine." Hope rolled her eyes. "Can I spend the night at your house?"

"Not tonight. I have students in the morning."

Thomas felt a tug at his heart. Carissa had said no, but Hope wasn't upset. She'd simply nodded, and the smile stayed in her eyes.

Once, small eyes had looked at him so trustingly. He swallowed hard and pushed back the memory where it belonged—in his past.

Chapter Three

Carissa tidied up the kitchen after dinner while Thomas sat with Katie and watched Jeopardy. He'd asked if he could help, but she'd shooed him away, claiming she needed her space.

What she'd needed was a few moments alone to breathe and collect her thoughts.

Her mind should have been on the business license application that needed to be finalized, the call to the insurance agent that was to have been returned, and the list she'd started of instruments she wanted to purchase. Scheduling meetings at the local schools and thinking of advertising should have been her main concerns. Instead, she was thinking about the man in the other room answering questions to some game show.

Since he'd come down the stairs that morning, her heart hadn't stopped racing.

That blond, disheveled hair and those blue eyes had burned into her mind. His soft voice, with the carefully chosen words, had her head spinning. It wasn't like her to see a man and have her skin grow hot, but she wasn't one to take her time either. She didn't want to complicate things with someone who was there to work with her, but she couldn't help but want to taste him.

"Katie says it's time for her medicine," he called. "I told her I'd come and get it."

When she heard his voice from the other room, she bit her lip. "It's in that cupboard. It's the little cup." She scrubbed a plate in the sink, trying to occupy her mind.

"You set it all up for her?"

"Yes. One time my aunt took her medicine three times because she couldn't remember that she'd taken it. She was in the hospital for a week."

"That's very thoughtful of you." He smiled before opening the cupboard door. He grabbed the cup and walked back out to Katie.

Carissa let out a breath. She thought about the night before when she'd turned and walked right into him. She'd felt his hands on her hips, his body pressed to hers, and his breath on her skin. God, she wished she'd just kissed him. She wished she'd pressed her lips to his. She wished she'd pulled him closer to her. Oh, if she'd only…

"Carissa." She gasped and spun around when Thomas said her name. He winked. "I'm sorry. I didn't mean to startle you."

"Just in deep thought, I guess."

"I'm going to head to bed. I think all my travels are catching up with me." He walked toward her. "Thank you for the day and for dinner. You're a wonderful cook."

"Thank you." She stuttered and nearly dropped the plate in the sink when she realized how close he stood to her.

"I'll be ready for that run and coffee before you start teaching tomorrow." He stepped closer and kissed her cheek. Carissa's breath hitched. "Goodnight." He left the whisper echoing in her ear.

Thomas admired Carissa from inside the house. She lifted one leg onto the railing of the porch and stretched over it. He could see plenty of her, and every part was toned and beautiful.

She wore a tiny pair of running shorts and a fitted shirt that clung to her curves. He bit his lip. A run was exactly what he needed now. Perhaps a run into an icy river. He squared his shoulders and joined her on the porch.

"Good morning. I thought you were a no-show." She smiled at him, and her eyes seared him. She'd pulled her long, dark hair back in a ponytail away from her face, and her eyes were larger, he swore it. She had full lips, the kind that a man could find pleasure in for hours. He shook it off.

"I didn't sleep too well," he said, and that wasn't a lie. Any sleep he had had been filled with dreams of Carissa.

"Me either." She reached for her sweatshirt that lay on the chair next to her. She tied it around her waist and looked into his eyes. "I kept thinking I should have kissed you when I ran into you the other night. It's sure made it hard to sleep lately." She winked and started down the steps.

Thomas's feet didn't move. Was she kidding? His heart was racing now, and he hadn't run a step. He wiped at the sweat that formed on his brow.

"Are you coming?" she called back to him from the street corner.

God, was she clueless as to what she'd just done? He took his first step and then another. Dear Lord, he was in trouble.

He never did run with her. It was much more like him following her. When she stopped in front of a diner, he was grateful. They hadn't run far, but he was certainly not in as good a shape as the woman he'd been chasing all the way from the house.

She stood with her arms over her head, stretching from side to side. Then she untied the sweatshirt from her hips and slid it over her arms.

Thomas finally caught up to her and immediately bent over with his hands on his knees. Carissa laughed. "I thought you could run."

"So did I. Sophia never ran that fast."

"Then she was taking it easy on you." She tightened the tail of hair at the back of her head. "Stand up."

"I can't." He panted as his vision went blurry, and all he could hear was the blood rushing in his ears.

She walked to him and pulled on his arms until she had them cuffed at the wrists and lifted over his head. "There. It lets in more air. You're just cutting off your oxygen by bending over."

He couldn't say anything. He just stood there staring at her glistening face and trying his damndest to suck in oxygen.

She was watching him carefully, and when his breathing began to settle, she smiled at him. "Feel better?" When he nodded, she tugged open the door of the diner. "Good, I'm hungry."

Thomas took in the atmosphere of the small diner. No one there seemed out of place. Some people were in suits. Some were in relaxed casual Saturday wear. A few looked like they hadn't seen a pillow yet. Others waved to the staff and other patrons as they headed out to a long, hard day of manual labor. The air filled with their voices and the smells of bacon and coffee. He'd missed such a place.

Carissa waved to the woman behind the counter and found a booth for them to sit in.

He followed, sitting across from her. "This place is great."

"This was always one of my favorite places to come to with my dad when I was growing up." She tossed her head from side to side, and he watched as she worked the tension from her neck.

"A hangout, huh?"

"It was one of his favorite places because he always came here with Sophia. He didn't tell me that until after I fell in love with her myself, or I would have protested and never have wanted to come here again."

She threw a menu his way and he opened it, glancing at the options.

"Didn't you always love Sophia? How could you not? She's amazing."

"Because when you're little and someone feeds you lines of BS about why your dad left, you tend to hate the person he's living with." She said it so matter-of-factly that he only nodded in agreement.

The waitress arrived at the table, and Carissa looked up at her with a smile. "Good morning, Betsy."

"Good mornin', honey. Got a new beau?" Thomas wiggled in his seat as she scanned her eyes over him. "Kinda skinny."

"You can fix that, right?"

Thomas grinned as he watched the two women banter.

"That would be my job." She winked.

They ordered, and Thomas tucked his menu back behind the napkin dispenser as Betsy walked away.

"What time is your first student?"

"Not until ten."

"But you dragged my butt out of the house at seven?"

"You run to breakfast. You take a nice stroll back." Yes, that did make sense. "Then home for a shower and off to work."

Suddenly his head filled with images of her in the shower. When he got home, his would have to be a cold one.

"I was giving some thought to the design of the school last night."

"You were?" Her brows knit, and he worried she wasn't open to criticism. But it would be better to add his opinion before all the interior walls were complete.

"I was thinking that back room is going to be awfully big. Don't you think you could put some tables in and room to do book work?"

"Book work?"

"Theory."

Carissa's beautiful, pouty lips thinned, and she shifted her glance out the window and then back toward him. "Theory goes home in a book and comes back for me to look over and put a sticker on. It's part of every lesson, but not meant for a class of its own. We want the kids to enjoy their classes, not dread them."

"I don't see why you don't—" Betsy interrupted with a plate of food, and the conversation on theory came to a halt. He watched as she doctored her breakfast with condiments, keeping her thoughts to herself.

Perhaps the discussion over theory would be best for another time. But time would soon be running out. He had opinions, and he damn well thought she should listen.

They ate their breakfast and managed to fill an hour with small talk, which did not include the curriculum of the school.

Thomas found Carissa intoxicating, once she'd stopped snarling at him. She was witty, funny, smart, and a little mouthy. What amazed him was how much she was like Sophia, though they'd never spent her childhood together for her to have adopted those traits and qualities.

"Well, look what the cat dragged in." A hand fell onto his shoulder, and he froze at the sound of David's voice.

"Daddy." Carissa jumped up to kiss her father on the cheek. "Where's Mom?"

"She headed over to Katie's to pick her up for her hair appointment. You know Katie. She won't miss it."

Hope sat next to Thomas, bouncing on the cushion of the booth. David gave her a look of warning, and she settled in even closer to Thomas.

David draped his arm over Carissa's shoulders. "So what are you two up to?"

Thomas felt the need to speak up. He'd done nothing but sit and have a meal with Carissa, but suddenly he felt as though he'd been caught doing something illicit.

Carissa spoke before he could begin to babble. "I made him go for a run before my first student."

"Yep, she's just like her mother," David confirmed.

"Not quite." Thomas shook his head as he looked at Carissa. "She runs faster."

Carissa threw her napkin at him. "We have to go. Want the booth?"

"Sure." David moved into the spot Carissa vacated. "It was nice to see you again, Thomas." He held his hand out as Thomas stood.

Thomas shook his hand. "Likewise. Goodbye, Hope. Enjoy your Saturday."

Carissa zipped up her sweatshirt as they walked away from the diner. "Are you okay?"

"I'm fine. I feel like I just got caught."

"Caught doing what?"

"I don't know. You run into someone's dad after you've just crawled out of bed with his daughter…" His eyes flew open, and he looked at her. "Wait, that's not what I meant. I meant separately. I mean…"

"Stop." She was laughing at him. Tears were forming in her eyes. "I got it." She laid her hand on his chest as she laughed. "Oh, Thomas, even if we'd crawled out of the same bed, he wouldn't have treated you any differently."

He wasn't too sure of that.

Carissa stepped closer to him until he could feel her body almost pressed to his. "You are too cute when you get flustered."

He reached for her hands before she could back away. "You're a forward one, aren't you?"

"Does it bother you?"

"No, I'm just not used to it. I'm a classical musician. I don't attract women's attention too often."

"I'm a classical musician, and I'm a woman. And when I see something I like, I go after it." She seductively bit her lip. "And I like you."

She moved up closer to him, and his entire body stiffened, as if to put up the wall he so desperately needed between them. "What is it you want, Carissa Kendal?"

"I don't know yet. Does that scare you?"

"Scares the hell out of me."

Her smile widened. "Well, by the pace of your heart…" She looked down at her hands that rested on his chest. "I'd say there's a mutual attraction."

"I'll go with that."

"And as I'm very selective with whom I share myself, don't think I'll be racing into your bed."

"Carissa, I didn't mean to assume that…"

She raised her finger to his lips. "But I'm certainly not one to take too much time either. You forget, I watched a man wait ten years for the woman he loves. One thing I'm not is patient." Her lashes fluttered, and his heart skipped another beat.

Thank God, he thought.

She stepped back and winked. "Well, we've come a long way in a few days. I guess, above all, we need to realize we still have to work with each other."

"True." Though he wondered how well it could go when she wouldn't even listen to his ideas.

"My business is too important to me to have something like a relationship with a coworker ruin it. My life is here in Kansas City, and my family, and now my business. I may not like to wait for things I want, but I don't like change much either."

Thomas swallowed the lump of fear that lodged in his throat from her words. No matter what happened between them, there would be change.

"Let's start by walking." She grabbed his hand and interlaced their fingers. "And talking."

"Talking?"

"Tell me who you are, Thomas Samuel." She turned her head toward him and narrowed her eyes. "And don't leave anything out."

If her forwardness hadn't ramped up his heart rate, her words would have. Where did he start? Did he start by telling her he was knocked around by his father until he was sixteen? That his father was an abusive, drunk bastard that finally killed one of his children in the fury of anger? Or did she want to hear how, after Pablo came out of the closet and he didn't have a job, he'd become an alcoholic like his father. That he'd almost killed himself and Pablo's lover, Pierre, one night in Paris? Is that what she wanted to know?

She gave his hand a gentle squeeze. "It's pretty simple, isn't it?"

He wished it were. "Do you want the basics like my birthday is January fourth? I'm thirty-three years old. You already know I've played the piano since I was three. Before moving here, which you also know I did only Thursday," he joked, trying to keep the conversation as light as possible, "I resided in a dinky apartment just outside of Rome." He took his free hand and ran it through his hair.

He really needed a haircut. "I didn't stick around to graduate high school. Not traditionally, at least. But Pablo made sure I had a high school diploma."

"You graduated high school in Italy?" He nodded. "Pretty cool."

He snorted a laugh. "Yeah, I guess so."

"Where were you born?"

"Maryland."

"First teacher's name?"

"Mrs. Norton."

"Color of your first bike?"

"Fire engine red."

"Name of your first pet?"

"Didn't have one."

She stopped and faced him. "Neither did I."

It was as if that was their connection. He squeezed his eyes shut. It was going to get too complicated too quickly, he could tell. Perhaps he should talk to Sophia about everything. He needed to make some decisions on how he wanted to handle Carissa Kendal. No matter what Carissa expected of him, he wasn't the marrying type, or a family man. He couldn't risk her losing her heart over him.

As they neared the house, he looked over at her. What if he lost his heart to her?

"I had a wonderful time." Carissa swung their hands between them as they walked up the front steps.

"So did I. I could get used to that every Saturday morning."

"Well, at least you're thinking about staying then."

His jaw dropped when she said that. For not wanting to make commitments, he sure was doing it.

Carissa unlocked the front door and walked inside the house. She kicked off her shoes, unzipped her sweatshirt, and shrugged out of it. With two fingers, she picked up her shoes and laid her sweatshirt over her arm. He noticed her routine. This was what she did every week, and now it included him.

"Time to get ready for work." She stepped closer to him. "How do we end our date?"

Sweat trickled down the back of his neck. He took a step closer to her and touched her cheek. He drew her toward him and gently laid a kiss on those full lips he'd been aching to caress with his own.

As he pulled back, her eyes remained closed. When she opened them, he was looking right into them.

"That was nice," she said on a sigh. "I'm guessing you're a great kisser."

"Maybe tonight we'll go on another date, and you can find out." He slid his hand from her cheek down her throat and lingered it there.

She raised her hand to his face, and it caught on his stubble. It was then he realized he needed to buy a razor.

As she pulled her hand away, it caught his attention. Quickly he grabbed her arm and turned it over, her inner wrist up.

"Holy cow." She pulled her arm away from him. "That had to hurt like hell."

Carissa's eyes flew open, and he knew defensiveness when he saw it. "Yeah, it did."

"What did you get it caught in?"

Her head tilted, and her expression softened. "What?"

"I said what did you get your arm caught in?" He reached for it and ran his fingers over her scar.

"I, um, I fell off my bike going down a hill."

"Got your arm stuck in the spokes?"

She nodded.

"Damn." He raised her wrist to his lips and kissed the scar.

"I have to get ready. I'll find you when I'm done, and we can make plans for tonight." She broke free from him and ran up the stairs to her room.

As soon as the door shut, Carissa paced the room and let the tears that had filled her eyes fall. Every emotion that could possibly be felt surged through her body. She was happy, sad, angry—and smitten to tie it all together. She sat down on the bed and rested her head in her hands.

In all the years she'd had that scar, no one had asked her what had happened in such a way. No, instead they had looked at it and made their own conclusions. Which still, to this day, made her angry. Anyone who'd been around her biological mother assumed they were the same. She'd tried to slit her wrists, so her daughter must have done the same damn thing. Then there was that school counselor. Carissa almost couldn't breathe.

She'd called her a liar and her father one as well. Convinced that he was covering for her, she'd threatened to take Carissa from her father. All because of the stupid scar on her wrist from a bicycle accident.

Sophia had scars, and they had bonded over them. They'd declared themselves warriors and never hid them again under necklaces, scarves, bracelets, or long sleeves. But pride in showing her scars didn't stop people from assuming she'd tried to end it all.

She let out a long, steady breath and let the sadness she felt from people not believing her drain away.

Then there was Thomas, who assumed nothing. She'd known Thomas Samuel going on three days, and already she was shedding tears over him, after having been fairly suggestive toward him. What had her mother done by bringing him into their lives?

Carissa sat up. Oh, dear God! She'd been set up. She set her jaw. What was Sophia thinking? Matchmaking was Katie and her Aunt Millie's game, not her mother's. Why would she think she needed to be set up?

At twenty-five, she was far from being a spinster. She'd had her share of relationships. Okay, so at best, she'd dated. But to call in a stranger... Carissa stood and paced the room again.

She'd heard stories about Thomas, sure. Not that she'd ever paid too much attention. Sophia only spoke to Carissa of the legendary Pablo, and those who toured with him, when they would sit and play their cellos together. Carissa knew it was Sophia's way of not bringing it up in front of her father. After all, for years he'd thought Sophia had left him for Pablo. It was a sore subject.

When Carissa had approached her mother about the school, her eyes lit up. "You'll need help," she'd said.

"I thought you'd help me."

"I'm busy with Hope. But I know someone who could use some roots, and he's one hell of a musician." In no time, Thomas Samuel was on his way back to the States to live. What kind of power did Sophia Kendal have over this man?

And now, what kind of power did he have over Carissa?

She certainly wasn't a winner in the relationship department. The last thing she wanted was a broken heart, and she'd been fairly successful in avoiding them. If things needed to be ended, she ended them. She wasn't about to pine for a man who didn't want her. However, she was fairly sure that Thomas Samuel wanted her. And likewise, she couldn't stop thinking she wanted much more from him than just to be smitten.

Carissa started pulling off her running clothes and throwing them into the laundry basket. She caught sight of the scar on her wrist. Damn, it had hurt. She ran her fingers over it. How she hadn't broken her arm she'd never know. A smile slipped across her lips. Thomas had noticed the scar, but it had taken three days, and when he saw it, he didn't assume. He didn't think she'd done something so horrible to scar herself. She sucked in a breath to steady herself. Things were going to be different with Thomas Samuel around.

Grateful that Carissa had loaned him her car keys, Thomas drove through town in search of a haircut.

He couldn't remember the last time he'd been in Kansas City. Maybe he'd never been. He laughed at himself. He was alone in a car, and he was laughing at himself. A year ago that would have been a sure sign he needed a drink. Even thinking about that now made his palms sweat.

"Keep it together, man," he warned himself as he came upon a barbershop. Just the sight of it had him wincing.

The last time he'd been in a barbershop, his father had dragged him there. He hadn't approved of the length of Thomas's hair and was bound and determined to make his point.

Thomas parked the car, squared his shoulders, and went inside.

There was a line of men on a bench, and all eyes turned to him when he walked through the door. He hung his jacket on the rack near the door. Instructions were called out to him to sit and wait, and he did.

Men came and went, and the line moved down the bench.

As the next chair opened, Thomas stood and started toward the space. At the same time, the door opened and a young man, perhaps fifteen years old, walked in and headed toward the open chair.

"What are you doing here? You have practice," the barber said to the boy.

"Didn't want to go. Thought I'd see if you needed help here."

"You think you can just miss practice and the coach will let you play? Go." He turned back to Thomas and nodded with his head for him to sit in the chair. Thomas sat as the man reached for a cape to drape over him.

"I'm not going back." The boy moved closer to the man, as if daring him to scold him more. "If you don't need my help, fine, but I don't care about basketball and I'm not going back."

The boy turned to walk out, but the barber grabbed his arm and swung him around. "Don't you dare talk to me like that."

Thomas sat only inches away. He could see the marks the man was making on the young boy's arm. His own arm began to ache from the memory of having been grabbed like that.

He swallowed hard and stood from the chair. "So, you play basketball?" His voice cracked as both sets of eyes turned toward him. "Great sport."

"No one asked for you to talk to my son." The barber stiffened his back, but kept his grip on his son.

"No, but I think you could let go of him and have a discussion rather than hurt him like you are."

The man let go of his son's arm and took a step toward Thomas. His heart began to race, and he could feel the sweat bead on his forehead. It had been a while since he'd been hit. He braced for it.

The man walked up to him until they were chest to chest. Thomas saw the fear in the young boy's face as he turned and ran from the shop.

"You have something to say?"

Thomas balled his fists at his sides. "I don't think you should touch him like that."

The barber kept his eyes directed on Thomas. He ran his tongue on the inside of his cheek, moving closer to Thomas until he nudged him backward.

"Why don't you get the hell out of here and never, ever come back."

Thomas sucked in a breath and stepped to the side, away from the chair. He noticed all eyes were on him, but he kept walking.

He released his fists and let the door slam behind him.

Perhaps he hadn't stopped the young boy from eventually getting beaten, but for that moment, the boy had gotten away.

He hurried to the car and fell into the seat behind the wheel. Breathing deeply, he tried to slow his heart rate. No child, no matter the age, deserved to be treated the way that man treated that boy or his father had treated him.

Trying to control his anger, he drove toward the mall. He'd just find one of those franchise places and get his haircut.

He emerged an hour later from the mall salon looking well-groomed, he thought. His nerves were still shaky, and his jaw hurt from grinding his teeth when he thought of the man. He didn't want to go back to the house in that state of mind, so he decided to walk around the mall to kill time before he returned.

He'd been only a moment from pounding his fist into the face of the man who'd made him so angry. The beer-gut-and-bar-fight build of the barber guaranteed he'd have beaten Thomas down, but it didn't matter. No one deserved to have children when he treated them like that.

He walked down the mall, looking in windows.

He gave it some thought. Only someone who couldn't control his anger would think of sticking his nose where it didn't belong and hitting a man over his own family business. He sucked in a breath. It was only proof that he was no better than his father. But the cycle would stop with him. He'd never have a child that he could pass on such a trait to. No, the anger and abuse stopped with him. It was the least he could do for humanity.

He continued his walk through the mall. Things had changed a lot in the eighteen years that he'd been away from the States. The mall crowd seemed so much younger than he'd remembered. When had he gotten so old?

There'd been a time he and Sophia would talk about what they'd missed stateside while living in Europe. There were stores, restaurants, scenic spots. She'd always kept a place in Seattle, but he'd never had one except for in Rome.

After a while, they didn't miss anything. Well, she missed David, he decided. Eventually she left everything to return to him, as she should have done much earlier in her career.

He stopped at the food court and bought a hot dog and soda. Even those standbys tasted so different from the ones in Rome.

He wasn't sure how long he'd sat in the food court watching people pass by him, but it amused him. Everyone had their own agenda. He recognized the men who were being dragged through the mall by the women that were three steps ahead of them. He recognized the woman on a mission. He'd seen that same expression on his mother's face a time or two. Then there were the teenage girls that were there to be seen and heard. He wondered if that was once Carissa.

Thomas tried to imagine her childhood.

He knew she'd showed up on David and Sophia's doorstep when she was very young. Sophia left to play with Pablo after that. He really didn't know about Carissa at all.

He took a sip of his soda, which had gone flat, and decided he'd been there longer than he'd thought. He tossed his trash in the bin and walked down the mall. He was tempted to buy something to make his room at Katie's homey. However, doing so would say he was laying down roots, and he wasn't sure he could commit to that. Sure, when Sophia had first called and offered him the chance to help start the school, he'd have bought land and built a house. Now, after spending a few days with Carissa, he couldn't make that kind of statement. Eventually he was going to break her heart and hurt her. He just hoped he could convince her to move on from any feelings he knew she was having before he did just that. Even worse, he was afraid he'd physically hurt her, and that had his stomach tied in knots, especially after the incident at the barbershop.

Outside a store window, he had to squeeze his eyes shut. In all his life, he'd never raised his hand to another human being. More than enough times, he'd been on the receiving end of it all, but never the giving. Yet how far did that have to travel in your blood before you did it? After all, he'd turned into a raging alcoholic and almost killed one of his dearest friends.

Pablo had destroyed his career in Rome for what he'd done to Pierre, and who could blame him? Sophia's call had come at the right time. He'd been without work for a long time, and without Pablo's support in the music community, Thomas was just a washed-up pianist. If Pablo could, he would bury Thomas's career completely.

"Thomas?" He heard his name called from behind him, and he snapped around to see Sophia and Katie slowly walking toward him. He adjusted his attitude and put on his best smile.

"I didn't mean to startle you," Sophia said as she approached him. "You looked deep in thought."

"I suppose I was."

"Are you doing some shopping?"

"Just killing time. Carissa is working, so she loaned me her car."

"All the better. She hates being interrupted when she works. Let's just say, there's a Jekyll and Hyde personality that comes out."

Thomas smiled. He knew others like that. Sophia, for one.

"So what are your plans for the rest of the day?" she continued.

"I think I'll drive around town and get acquainted a bit. Maybe you could give me directions to the school, and I could stop by and help David."

Sophia nodded and began to look through her purse for a pen and a piece of paper.

"I think Carissa and I are going to go to dinner tonight." He said it as nonchalantly as he could, but Sophia's head snapped up.

"Really?" Her eyes opened wide, and a smile slid across her lips. "I heard she dragged you out for a run to The Spot for breakfast, too."

"That she did. She runs faster than you ever did."

Sophia laughed and went back to writing out directions to the school on the back of a receipt.

"Okay, here are directions from the mall and then directions back home."

"You know me too well, dear friend."

"I hope so."

Thomas took his instructions, said his goodbyes, and headed back down the mall toward the parking lot.

Katie scanned her granddaughter's face. "Sophia, what are you doing?"

"Nothing, Grandma."

Katie smiled with a shake of her head. "Well, at least I taught you well. Matchmaking is an art, and you can't meddle too much or it gets sloppy."

"I agree. Carissa's smarter than I am and has a stronger will. He'll be either in or out, but by the sounds of it, he's in."

"I raised a hopeless romantic." Katie began pushing her walker down the mall and Sophia followed, laughing.

"No, Grandma, I'm a hopeful romantic."

David walked out of the building toting a two-by-four as Carissa's car pulled up in front and parked. He was sure she was there to check up on his progress. She'd already called three times. When he saw Thomas climb from the driver's seat and Carissa wasn't with him, mild apprehension rose in his belly.

"Hey." He gave Thomas a nod as he headed to the chop saw set up just outside the door and set the board on the saw's table. He pulled the pencil from behind his ear and darkened the line he'd made inside earlier. "Did you come to offer a hand?"

"Well, I'll be the first to admit I'm not much of a handy kind of guy, but I thought I'd come by and see what I could help out with. Carissa has students all day. I'd just be in her way."

David chewed on the inside of his cheek and considered him with a nod.

"Cutting that board or taking a break?" Jeremy walked outside and stopped, scanning a look over Thomas. "Oh, hi."

"Jeremy, this is Thomas." David lined up the blade with the pencil mark.

Jeremy stuck his hand out, and Thomas shook it. "So, are you here to help this loser build this wall?"

"Loser?" David smirked and nodded in Jeremy's direction. "You do see the man here covered in sawdust. He must be a loser, too."

Jeremy gave Thomas a slap on the back. "C'mon inside. We'll put you to work."

David followed them with the board he'd just cut.

Thomas's voice carried from the back. "I'm trying to convince her that we need a classroom for theory."

David walked to the back of the school where the two men stood looking at the empty space.

Jeremy's eyebrows drew together. "Theory?"

David laughed. "Those little black dots on the paper."

"Smart ass." Jeremy looked at Thomas. "Notes. I know what the hell notes are." He shook his head at David. "Why does she need a room for that? Aren't they just learning how to play?"

"Dear God, you have no idea." David patted Jeremy on the back. "You'd better stop while you're ahead." He shifted his glance toward Thomas. "As soon as she says she wants a room for theory, I'll build it for her." But not a second sooner, he thought.

By the time they decided to stop for the day, they'd erected the partition wall that would separate the parents' area from the rest of the school. Though Thomas had been correct about not being handy, David was grateful for the extra set of hands.

"Thanks for your help," he called with a wave as he locked the front door, and Thomas climbed into Carissa's car and drove away.

Jeremy tossed his tool belt into the back of his pickup. "So that was Thomas?"

"Yep."

"Mary Alice talked about him for an hour last night."

David secured the tailgate of the pickup and let his grip linger on the metal. "What did she have to say?"

"Just that they had eyes for each other."

"Eyes?" His voice shot up in pitch.

"Yep." He nodded. "Said they didn't take their eyes off each other. Laughed easily. Touched."

"Touched?"

"Christ, you pansy. She's twenty-five." Jeremy laughed as he walked toward the driver's door and pulled it open. "You left her alone in that house with that man, and you're scatterbrained if you think they're just smiling at each other." Jeremy laughed, and David backed away from the back of the truck as he pulled away.

David walked to his car and thought of them earlier that morning at breakfast. They did look very comfortable together. He shook his head. He wasn't quite ready to think about his little girl getting involved with anyone. Especially the man she was living with, as Jeremy had so thoughtfully reminded him. He knew all too well that those rooms weren't quite far enough apart in the house that once had been a boarding house with rules, but was now just a home shared by a healthy young man, David's attractive daughter, and an old woman who had done her share of matchmaking.

Chapter Four

David moved in behind Sophia as she folded the sheets from the basket of laundry perched on the kitchen table and placed a kiss on her neck. She leaned in against him with a sigh.

"Carissa just called. They'll both be here tomorrow for dinner."

"How's Thomas settling in?"

"Pretty well. She said they were going to dinner tonight. I think she's taken him under her wing already. And I do believe they're a little smitten with each other." She confirmed what Jeremy had said to him with her wide smile.

"Sophie, I don't know about this. I don't even know this guy." In an attempt to keep his composure and his hands calm, he reached into the basket, pulled out a pillowcase, and folded it.

"David, I wouldn't have called him if I thought he'd bring harm to Carissa or wasn't good for the school. I want this to succeed for her. It's what she's always wanted."

"I just don't like you putting my daughter out there like this." He saw her wince and wished he could retract the words.

"Our daughter," she corrected him with narrowed eyes. She might as well have punched him in the gut. "And I would never have do anything to harm her in any way. You should know that better than anyone."

David laid the pillowcase on the table and walked back around behind his wife. He slipped his arms around her waist and rested his chin on her shoulder. "I know. It's just that when Carissa takes on a project, she dives right in. She doesn't take her time to see things through and to be patient."

"You think she'll fall in love too fast?"

"Fall in love?" His temper was rising as he moved away from his wife and paced the kitchen. "You did plan this out." He wiped his sweating hands on the sides of his pants. "You already have her married off." He flung his hands into the air. "What the hell happens if she falls in love with him and he doesn't with her? What then? They still have to work together. You moved the man over here from Rome, and he has nothing. If this doesn't work out, maybe you've ruined his life."

Sophia stood before him, her mouth open. "I don't want her to waste years of her life. I wasted three years thinking your proposal was enough, but not accepting it. I wasted another ten trying to figure out my life while you were here waiting."

"I wasn't waiting. I was raising Carissa," he reminded her.

"Then you should know she's smarter than both of us." She dropped the folded sheets into the basket. "I love them both. Carissa is my daughter. Thomas is my friend. They are two of the most talented people on this planet, and by God, if they've already found each other, that's great. If they're not interested, they won't think a thing about it. Dammit, David, don't shut the door on her. She's been in love before and had it fall apart. She's not going to break.

"So I introduced her to a wonderful man, who I think the world of. What's wrong with that? I knew two old ladies that did the same thing once. Imagine that conversation—'I have a granddaughter...I have a nephew.'" She blew out her breath as he watched her gather her composure and the basket of laundry. Without another word, she walked out of the kitchen.

Carissa spun into the kitchen, making a grand entrance. She'd wiggled into a pair of dark jeans and accented them with a pair of high heels. The low-cut, red blouse immediately had Thomas's attention, she noticed. She'd fastened the Saint Nicholas pendent her mother had given her around her neck, and it dangled between her breasts. "I'm ready."

"You look beautiful." He stood from his seat at the table, making a visible effort not to let his gaze dip lower than her face.

"Thank you." She slipped on her jacket. "Katie, will you be all right? Do you need anything?"

"Just for the two of you to get out of here so I can turn on the television and enjoy my peaceful night."

"We'll be home around ten. Call my cell phone if you need anything."

"Go. You hover more than your father, do you know that?" Katie stood and reached for her walker.

"Yeah, well, I was taught by the best."

"Yes, you were. Now go."

Carissa led the way out the back door, and Thomas pulled the door shut behind them.

"She doesn't like to be fussed over, does she?"

"Yes, she does. She just doesn't want you to think she does. If she didn't like it, she would have moved to a retirement home years ago and gone chasing some old man. As it is, she was glad to have Aunt Millie around, and now she's glad to have me around."

Thomas opened the door for her. His cologne tickled her feminine senses. He was cleanly shaven, well dressed, and God, he was handsome. The shorter haircut made him look even more virile, if that were possible.

Carissa stood there a moment and looked into his eyes. "You know what would start this date off right?"

"What would that be?"

She reached her hand behind his neck and brought his head toward her. "If we start with a kiss."

There wasn't a moment to protest, even if he'd had the mind to do so. She had those full lips brushing against his, but it wasn't just a peck. Her mouth opened to his, and her tongue sought his out as her other arm pulled him tight to her body.

Thomas had never had a kiss that had him lightheaded, but the one Carissa was planting on him was doing just that. His arms wound around her waist and pulled her to him, pressing their bodies tight to each other.

She wasn't letting up. One of her hands was in his hair, while the other slid over his chest. The knot in his belly was as tight as the pressure in his slacks. When she finally released his lips, she balanced her forehead against his. "I knew you were a good kisser."

"You're not too bad yourself," he said with an unsteady breath.

"Thomas," she began. With her head still pressed to his, she shifted her eyes to meet his and continued, "I'd really like more of that."

He made a moan of some kind to indicate that his thoughts were on the same path.

Carissa closed her eyes. She didn't release her grip, but took in a deep breath before opening her eyes and gazing at him.

"I want to make something clear. I know what I'm doing. I'm not a child. When I want something, I go after it." She lifted her head. "Thomas, I want you."

"Carissa."

"Don't say anything." Her finger pressed to his lips. "I know we haven't even started working together, but in the last couple days, the things you've done to me by just being near me have sent my head spinning." The hand on the back of his neck slid toward his cheek. Her perfume filled his head. Her eyes settled right into his. "After dinner, I want to take that kiss further." She molded her body harder to his. "I want to make love to you."

He knew he gasped aloud by the widening of her eyes, but he didn't release her. He wasn't sure he could physically walk away from her at that moment. "Carissa, you don't know me." At the moment, he didn't know himself. That was what this trip was about. Finding himself without hurting anyone in the process. How come she kept putting herself in his path?

Carissa touched his lips with a brush of her fingers. "But I want to know you." She straightened, released herself from him, and ducked into the car.

He shut the door, noticing her wanting eyes were still on him. How was it he finally landed the job of a lifetime and with it a woman he dreaded hurting for any number of reasons—but couldn't turn down?

The hostess greeted them at the door and escorted them to a booth that would seat four. Carissa scooted to sit at the place setting right next to Thomas. She liked having him that close. Candles lit the darkened room, and soft music set the mood for romance.

She felt her skin get hotter with him near her. She rested her hand on his leg and felt him straighten. She realized she might be a bit much for him, but she'd never been so attracted to a man in all her life. She wanted this one, and with every minute that passed, she realized she wanted him for keeps.

"How about a bottle of wine?" Her voice was low and husky.

"How about a glass for you, and I'll have water," he said with a dip of his head, his voice soft as though he were saying it in secret.

She considered him a moment. "Designated driver?"

"Not much of a drinker."

Carissa scanned the menu. She wasn't the least bit hungry—for food. She wished the waitress would come to the table. Studying the menu wasn't what she wanted to be doing with her eyes.

The waitress finally arrived at the table and offered the specials for the evening. Carissa considered them, then ordered her wine and dinner, and relaxed next to him, hoping to find out more about the man who was stealing her heart piece by piece. "Are you always quiet or just around women?" she asked from behind the rim of her wine glass as the candle on the table flickered.

Thomas adjusted his shoulders, squaring them. "I get pretty quiet around women who have me thinking thoughts I shouldn't be thinking."

Carissa inched even closer to him. "I love that I'm driving you wild."

"You'll hate me next week," he promised, lifting his water glass to his lips. Carissa shook her head.

"I hope not." She sat back. "What worries you? Do you think I can't work with you if I seduce you?"

"Let's just say I'm not the kind of man…women don't want men like me."

Carissa wasn't sure why he was so afraid of her, but it wasn't going to stop her.

"I think women like you just fine. Let's get to know each other. I think you'll find it hard to turn me down." She drank down her wine. Feeling it swim in her head, she let the smile settle on her lips. She was making him nervous, and it was a thrilling feeling.

By the time they finished eating, she didn't know much more about the man, but he had her tuned up. His eyes smoldered in the dark booth. He told stories of places he'd been and people he'd met. He stole a kiss after stealing a bite of cheesecake from her fork, and she trembled. He spoke to her in Italian, and her pulse raced.

As she watched him, a knot tightened in her belly. This man was going home and falling into bed with her, so help her God!

Hand in hand, they left the restaurant and stepped out into the cool evening air. It wasn't even close to the cold shower Thomas would need when they got home. No matter what Carissa said, he couldn't take her to bed. There was a fine line, and he couldn't cross that line no matter how badly he wanted to. "Why don't we take a little walk?"

"A walk?" Disappointment dripped in her voice.

"Yeah, I think we need a walk." It was perhaps a bit cooler than he'd thought, but he tugged her along.

She hugged up to his arm. "Are you afraid to be alone with me?"

"I'm man enough to say yes."

"Thomas," she stopped and looked up at him, "what are you afraid of?"

He gathered her hands in his and held them to his chest. "Carissa, I'm not the marrying kind."

"I didn't know I was asking."

"You deserve better than me. I'll hurt you."

"Then don't." The glimmer in her eyes was fading, and that began to break his heart. "What if I hurt you?"

He smiled. "Why would you do that?"

"C'mon, I think we're on equal ground. Who's to say one of us isn't going to break the other's heart? I'm a professional, and I thought you were, too. We're going to work together, that's a given." He wished he could control the rapid pace of his heart when she laid her hands on his chest. "For the time being, we're even going to live together." Her eyebrows gave a playful rise. "It's been a long time since I've been with a man I find not only as attractive as you, but that I'm completely comfortable around." She pushed her body up against his, and he could feel the warmth radiate from her.

"You're not going to back down, are you?" With her that close, he couldn't help but reach his hands into her hair.

"No," she said as she rose on her toes and took his mouth with hers.

The air around them grew colder, but the heat between them sizzled. He pulled her closer. Urgency burned through his core, and he knew he had to get her home before he ripped her clothes off right on the street.

They collected the car and started home. Now that it had started, he was having a hard time keeping his hands to himself. His lips wandered down her neck and over her ear as she drove.

"Thomas." Her voice was airy, and he tugged on her ear with his teeth. "I can't—concentrate this—way."

"Then drive faster," he said, and she laughed.

The moment they hit the driveway she killed the engine and flew into his arms. His hands tangled in her hair, pulling her closer as his tongue explored her mouth. His hands slipped through her jacket. He tugged her blouse loose, and his hands roamed over her warm skin. She moaned, which drove him mad.

When he cupped her breast and gave it a squeeze, she gasped. The soft sound sent his body into overdrive. He had to get her into the house, on a flat surface, against a wall, anywhere where there wasn't the obstacle of the center console.

"We have to get inside." He moaned against her lips.

"I don't know if I can wait that long." She worked the buttons on his shirt.

The glow of lights moved down the street.

"Wait. Wait." He pulled back.

Sirens blared, approaching fast.

They adjusted themselves quickly and climbed from the car as a fire truck and an ambulance pulled up in front of the quiet house. Only a moment later, her parents' car screeched to a stop behind the fire truck.

They both flew from their car.

"Oh, my God! What's wrong?" Carissa was running to her father as Sophia ran through the front door of the house.

David grasped her shoulders and glanced over her disheveled appearance and then at Thomas's before looking back at Carissa. "Katie. She fell."

"Oh, God." She covered her mouth and broke from her father's grasp to run into the house.

Paramedics had Katie on the gurney by the time Thomas made it into the house. Carissa was already at her side.

"Oh, I should have been here. I should have stayed with you." She cried as her mother put her arm around her.

"I'll be fine," Katie assured her as they moved her through the house.

The words were confident, but Thomas couldn't help but notice how weak Katie's voice sounded. Carissa collapsed against Sophia. "I should have stayed. I should have been here for her."

"She would have been mad if you canceled your dinner. Besides, it could have happened with you here just as easily.

She was in bed. She was getting up to go to the bathroom. You can't blame yourself."

"I need to go with her. I need to be with her." Carissa pulled away and stumbled toward the door.

Thomas took a step toward Sophia and laid a gentle hand on her arm. He was in unfamiliar territory. Compassion wasn't something he'd witnessed in his life too often. Watching the women comfort one another, he wished he could offer some. "Sophia, go with her. You can leave Hope with me. I'll look after her."

"That would be wonderful. Thank you," Sophia patted his hand as she walked Carissa out of the house.

David carried in Hope, who was sound asleep. He laid her on the couch and draped an afghan over her. "Are you sure about this?"

"It's the least I can do." He looked at David, whose brows were creased. Thomas realized his shirt was still unbuttoned, and his hair was a mess. The feeling of being caught with Carissa was worse than he'd imagined when he'd seen David at the restaurant. "Katie will be all right, won't she?"

David shrugged. "She's tough. We'll call you."

Thomas nodded and watched as David left the house.

He sat quietly, watching the small girl on the couch breathe in and out. Her eyes darted beneath her eyelids as she dreamed. She reminded him of his own sister, so sweet, so innocent. The thought tugged at him uncomfortably. He missed his sister. Envy surged through him when he thought of the relationship Carissa had with Hope. He'd been a part of a relationship like that once. But those days were long gone.

Thomas turned on the television, and the glow filled the dark room. He turned the sound to a whisper so it wouldn't disturb Hope. He watched for a few minutes, but his body refused to be still.

His fingers itched to move. He'd noticed the piano in the study, pushed against the wall. Obviously it was there more for the purpose of lessons than for decoration, but it was late, and he didn't want to wake Hope. He longed to touch the keys, to make music now when he didn't know what else to do.

He walked to the study and shut the door.

He rested his fingers on the keys and let them slide along them without a sound. The song he'd play wouldn't be joyful or beautiful. It would be painful and mournful. That was how he felt.

Thomas walked to the kitchen and found a bowl and a cup in the sink. He washed them and set them on the counter to dry, then wiped down the already spotless counters to keep his hands occupied. Soon he moved from the kitchen to the hallway where he could see Katie's bedroom. The light on the nightstand was still on. He entered the room cautiously and picked up the few items that had fallen to the floor with Katie. He arranged her slippers on the side of her bed and pulled the sheets and quilts up to tidy the space. Then he turned off the light and headed back toward the living room.

Hope was awake. She sat very still on her great-grandmother's couch and looked at the television through sleep-hazed eyes. She wasn't startled when Thomas entered the room. She looked up at him and then back at the television. "Do you understand them?"

"What?" He looked at the television and realized he'd been watching an Italian movie. He smiled. "Yes, I understand them."

"What language are they speaking?" She pulled her legs under her and wrapped the blanket around her.

"It's Italian." He took his seat in the chair by the couch again. "That's what they speak in Italy."

"That's where you came from?"

"That's where I was living."

He watched her as she watched the movie for a few more minutes.

"How come you can understand them, but I can't?"

"I lived in Italy a very long time. You learn the language when you live somewhere long enough."

"Will you teach me Italian?"

"Maybe I can teach you some words."

Hope stood from her seat on the couch and walked toward him with the afghan dragging behind her. She stopped in front of him and made a move to sit on his lap. Thomas tensed, and Hope climbed up on him, laying her head on his shoulder and draping her feet over the side of the chair.

Thomas covered her with the afghan and did his best to settle into the chair with her.

Perhaps she needed comfort. Perhaps she was cold or scared. He wasn't sure, but she seemed to trust him and he wasn't going to break that trust.

"Is Grandma going to be okay?" Her voice was muffled against his shirt.

"I'm sure she will be. Your dad said he'd call." He ran his hand over her soft, blonde hair, and she snuggled closer with a yawn.

"Grandma is very old."

"Yes, she is."

"Someday she'll die."

Thomas swallowed hard. Someday they all would die, he thought. Some would die from old age like Katie, some to disease like their Aunt Millie, and some by the hands of hateful others. "I don't think that'll be soon. You have to think positive thoughts," he offered, and he heard her sniffle.

"Aunt Millie died." The comment was simply stated. "Mandy died."

"Who's Mandy?" He ran his hand down her hair again. Though he was trying to soothe her, he also found comfort in it.

"My mother."

Thomas felt his breath hitch. He wouldn't ask. That wasn't right. Yet that one sentence had so many things running through his head. Wishing Carissa were there, he closed his eyes and took a moment to enjoy the feeling of someone needing him for comfort the way Hope was. Who was this misplaced child that ended up in Sophia's hands? What a gift, he thought. What a gift.

He felt her become heavy against him and realized she'd fallen asleep. He managed to pull the lever on the side of the chair and raise his feet. The movie on the television still played out in Italian, and he listened to the words that were as familiar to him as English. Soon he drifted to sleep.

It wasn't until he heard the opening of the front door that Thomas's eyes flew open. He quickly felt the numbness of his arms and realized Hope still slept on his lap. The television now played a French movie, which he understood as well as the Italian one. David's weary face appeared in the shadows of the television light.

"Sorry to wake you," he whispered.

"No." Thomas tried to wake himself up to be more alert. "No problem."

"I should have called, but Sophia and Carissa were a wreck. Trying to calm them kept me occupied." He ran his hands over his face. "I hope she wasn't any trouble."

"Not at all." He tried to make his body to move, but found it impossible after having held her for so long.

Hope stirred on his lap and woke up when she heard her father's voice call her name softly. She smiled and slowly crawled off Thomas's lap.

"C'mon, let's get you home." David tucked the afghan around her and held her to him as she gathered her bearings. "Carissa is going to stay at the house tonight. Will you be all right here alone?"

"Sure, I'll be fine. Is Carissa okay now?"

"She's fine. I think this shook her up. When Millie died, she'd fallen too and didn't recover."

"But Katie's okay, right?" There was desperation in his voice as he tried to stand to talk to the man before him.

"She'll be okay. They're going to keep her for a few days. They thought she'd broken her hip, but it looks like she's just banged up a little."

Thomas nodded. That was good news, he decided. David offered a tired smile. "Thanks for watching her."

"My pleasure."

Thomas walked them to the door.

David opened the screen to let Hope out. She took a few stumbling steps, then stopped and turned back around. She wrapped her arms around Thomas's legs and gave him a tight squeeze.

He watched them drive away and then closed the front door and fell to the floor behind it.

Hope would never know what her sincerity did to him.

He buried his face in his hands. Sarah had hugged him like that and trusted him to protect her. How could he have let her down?

Chapter Five

Thomas woke in a cold sweat. He sat straight up in bed. His heart was pounding in his chest and his breath was unsteady.

He ran his fingers through his wet hair and took a few deep cleansing breaths. The sun was peeking through the drawn curtains. The throbbing in his head felt like he'd indulged all night with a bottle of whisky, but he hadn't. It took him a moment to remember he'd shared a beautiful evening with a beautiful woman and just how chaotic the night had become.

He rested his aching head in his hands. The night hadn't quite ended as he'd thought it would have, even if he'd promised himself he wouldn't go there. How had he gone from a wonderful dinner with Carissa to feeling her up in the car like a teenager to holding her baby sister all night?

The emotional shifts had him uneasy; he was tired and run down, and that had brought on the dreams.

He swallowed hard as he lay back on his pillow. His throat was sore. That meant he'd been yelling in his sleep. Thank God, Carissa had stayed at her parents' house.

He pressed his fingers to his eyes. It was still so vivid in his head. Screaming, pain, and the dark places he'd hidden. His mother's yelling, his father's yelling, and his sister's sudden silence made him nauseous. He kicked his feet over the side of the bed and headed to the bathroom to run water over his face. He needed coffee.

The throbbing in his head began to dull, and it was then he could hear the noises that filled the house. Carissa was home. She was playing her cello. From the sound of the music, she was in a miserable mood.

Thomas gave his teeth a quick brush, pulled on his pants, threw on a sweatshirt, and headed down the stairs. Barefooted, he stood just outside the study door. It was open, and her back was to him. She wore a pair of lounge pants and a tank top. Her hair was wet. How long had she been home? When had he had the worst of his nightmare? He ran his fingers through his hair again. It didn't feel the same as it had for months when he'd needed a haircut. He realized everything in his life was changing, right down to his hair. He stood silently and listened to her play.

She wasn't playing something soft and warm. No, she was playing the song he'd come to despise, even as he'd helped write the notes down on the paper. She was using the music to relieve the stress. He'd done it himself many times. Her body moved into the instrument. Her fingers pinched the strings, and her hand gripped tight to the bow. He slipped into the room and headed to the piano. His hands were still itching to play. He started in the middle of the piece, where she was playing, blending his notes with hers.

Her head shot up. Obviously she hadn't heard him come into the room. He caught her eye, but never took his fingers off the keys. She put her bow back to the strings and played.

Carissa's music was before her, but he knew she didn't need it to play. Thomas would never need the music for the piece. Not only had he helped write it, he'd played it so many times he probably hummed it in his sleep. He hated it, though it was a beautiful piece and the people of the world seemed to embrace it. Even alone in the room with Carissa and their instruments, he could hear Pablo DiAngelo belt out the words in Italian.

When the piece had ended, he didn't turn from the keys right away. He took a deep breath and closed his eyes because he could feel hers on him.

"We play well together," she said.

"You're an amazing, amazing woman, Carissa." He turned to see her standing still, holding the neck of the cello in one hand and her bow in the other.

Her eyes were open wide. She tucked her lips between her teeth and looked at the floor. "I play that when I'm trying to cool down. I played it for first chair my senior year. I got it. Sophia helped me with it."

"She's an amazing woman, too." He leaned back against the piano and crossed his arms over his chest.

Carissa nodded. She turned and set the cello in the case that lay across the large, oak desk in the corner. "They're going to have to put Katie in an assisted living home, you know." Her voice had hitched, and he knew tears were soon going to spill over.

"She's ninety-two years old, Carissa. She needs more than what you can offer her. She'll be fine."

Carissa nodded in agreement. "I wanted to stay, but she kicked me out." The slightest laugh escaped. "Called me a spoiled brat and told me to go home to my man." He heard what he assumed was supposed to be humor, but she had swallowed back the chuckle with a sob.

Thomas walked up behind her and rested his hands on her shoulders. He felt her tremble. "You went home with your father," he reminded her as he breathed in the scent of her shampoo.

"I was afraid to come back here." She turned to face him. "She said go home to my man. She meant you. She…"

What time was there to think before his mouth come down on hers? He parted her welcoming lips with his, and his tongue sought out hers as his hands slipped around her waist and pulled her closer to him. There was heat, just like the interrupted kiss the night before. He nipped at her lower lip with his teeth, then skimmed over her jaw and neck. She tossed her head back to give him access to her throat as he pushed his body harder to hers.

His hands filled with her. Christ, what he wanted to do to her at that very moment. His head was still spinning, and he was pushing thoughts from it. He would not begin to take her in that very room, like his head and body wanted to do. Hell no, she deserved more. Then again, she deserved more than him.

The sweet taste of her sent him back to her mouth, his fingers wrapped up in her long, dark, wet hair.

Carissa couldn't still her hands. She ran them under his sweatshirt and up the smooth skin of his back. God, why didn't he begin feeling his way over her body? She wanted him, right then and right there. When he pulled from her and rested his forehead to hers, she sighed. The sound was an angry one.

The phone rang, and with Katie in the hospital, she couldn't ignore it. She pulled away from him and stepped into the hallway to pick up the phone on the table.

She spoke to her mother, aware that Thomas was leaning up against the door listening. With a cleansing breath, she turned around to see him watching her, and her heart flipped in her chest. Oh God, she couldn't believe he was there. So fresh from sleep, so fair, so desperately trying to talk himself out of loving her. She could see it in his eyes. She'd seen it before.

She stood a moment longer and watched him watching her as she hung up the phone. He wanted her. There had been no mistaking that feeling when he pushed up against her. She feared he wanted more, but wouldn't give it. The expression in his eyes matched that of her birth mother, though she assumed Thomas had a different inward battle brewing. He didn't want to love her and hurt her. Her birth mother just hadn't wanted to love her.

"They're coming for me in a few minutes and heading to the hospital." She fidgeted with her hair, pulling it back with her hands and letting it fall down her back. "We're having dinner at my parents' house tonight," she added.

"I remember."

"I'd better get dressed." She stumbled past him and up the stairs.

"Carissa, leave me directions to the hospital, and I'll meet up with you when I get showered and shaved. I'd like to see her too, if you don't mind."

She turned toward him and smiled at him, pleased that the man who seemed to be fighting a personal battle of compassion had found some for her grandmother, whom she adored. "I think she'd really appreciate that."

With coffee brewed, Katie's room number, and directions to the hospital in his hand, Thomas wandered upstairs, showered, and shaved. He pulled out his beige slacks and a crisp, white shirt. He was sure there would be somewhere he could pick up some flowers for Katie on the way to the hospital.

He bought her a beautiful bouquet of red roses at a grocery store he passed. He knew they'd bring a smile to her lips. For Carissa, he purchased a single pink bud, hoping to elicit the same response from her.

Carissa's directions were not as clear as those her mother had shelled out at the mall to get him around town, but with a U-turn and a slight detour, he found the hospital.

A man and a child climbed into the elevator with him. The boy, he figured, was about three. He held a bear in one arm and a strangled flower in the other. The man looked tired, as though he'd had no sleep for days. He, too, carried flowers in the crook of his arm.

The little boy looked up at Thomas. "Are you taking those to a mommy, too?"

"No, to a grandma."

"I'm going to see my mommy. She had a baby. I have a sister. She's ugly, but Mommy says she'll get prettier. But I don't know."

"Little girls do get prettier, I promise," Thomas said, and the father gave him a thankful smile for the boost to the boy.

"Her name is Simone."

"That's pretty."

"What would you name a little girl?"

"Thomas, that's enough," his father said to him.

With a whisper, Thomas looked down at the little Thomas. "My name is Thomas, too."

"Just like the train, huh?"

"Yeah, I guess so." The doors opened, and Simone's big brother, Thomas, walked out with his father's hand on his back.

The exchange tugged at Thomas's heart. He once was big brother Thomas to a little baby girl. She'd turned out to be pretty, just like he'd promised little Thomas his sister would.

He was a bit uneasy as he strode toward Katie's room. When he got there, he found he was alone with her, and she was sleeping. He found a slip of paper, wrote a little note, and laid it next to the flowers. When he turned back around, Katie was sitting up looking at him, and she smiled. The flowers had done their job, he decided. "I thought you were asleep."

"I'm getting plenty of that around here."

"How are you?"

"Oh, hell, I'm fine. They just like to fuss over me, like my granddaughters do."

"They love you." Thomas gathered the flowers and walked to her bedside. "I got these for you."

"They sure are lovely." She reached out and touched a petal. "Sophia brought a vase and tucked it in the closet. She must have known a handsome man would bring flowers today. Just put them in there."

He nodded and looked for the vase.

"Grandma, I got the magazine you wanted." Carissa fluttered into the room. "I talked to the nurse, and she's going to bring you—" She stopped when she noticed Katie's eyes shift toward Thomas, who watched her in the mirror over the sink. "I didn't know you were here."

"Just got in. Brought this beautiful woman some beautiful flowers," he said as he turned with the roses shoved into the vase.

"They're lovely." Carissa's cheeks flushed the color of the roses, and a sliver of a smile crossed her beautiful lips.

Katie watched the two of them make small talk to her, as if they didn't want to talk to each other. As if they didn't want her to know there were feelings between them. But Katie was no fool. She was an expert when it came to seeing what others didn't.

"You know, I'm tired again. Why don't the two of you get out of here?" She adjusted herself on the bed.

"Are you okay?" Carissa's voice quivered as the nurse entered the room.

"Hell, I'm fine. Just want you all to leave me be. Tell your mama to go home, too. Just go have some fun."

"Okay, I'll go find them in the cafeteria." Carissa planted a kiss on Katie's cheek. "I have my—"

"You have that silly phone, and I'll call you if I need you. Shoo!"

Carissa gathered her purse and started out the door.

"Take care, Katie." Thomas took her hand and kissed it, then pulled back to follow Carissa, but Katie caught his sleeve and pulled him back down.

"Take care of her," she said with a wink.

"I will." Thomas sealed his promise with a smile and followed Carissa out of the room.

"That's my granddaughter," Katie held out her arm for the nurse to lace a blood pressure cuff around it.

"She's beautiful."

"She is, isn't she?" Katie relaxed. "They're getting married soon."

"That's wonderful. How long have they been engaged?"

"Oh, they're not. They don't know they're in love yet, but soon. Very soon."

Carissa called Sophia to give her Katie's instructions. She smiled as she could hear Sophia give a hushed curse.

"I'm leaving with Thomas. We'll see you tonight." She tucked her phone back into her purse and touched his arm, enjoying the way his breath caught. "It was nice of you to come by and see her."

"I feel like she's this legend, and I finally got to know her. I'm starstruck."

"She's everything to my mother and to me."

"I know." He took her hand and interlocked their fingers. She looked up at him and smiled.

"What do you say we head over to the school and pound some nails? I really feel like that would lift my mood right now."

Thomas laughed. He really needed to remember to pack extra clothes for spur-of-the-moment manual labor.

"Sure." He opened the door for her to climb in behind the wheel, and she stopped.

"What's this?" She lifted the single, wrapped rose from the seat.

"It's for you."

"Thank you." She lifted the bud to her nose. "You're full of surprises, aren't you?"

Thomas rocked back on his heels and shoved his hands into his pockets.

"C'mon, let's go." A simple comment and he had suddenly become uneasy. What surprises did Thomas still have? As much as he was taking over her every thought, she knew so little about him.

"Just a second." She laid the rose on the dash and turned to him. "I want to thank you properly." Carissa raised her arms around his neck and pulled herself up to him. She skimmed her lips over his as his hands slipped down her sides and settled on her hips.

The kiss wasn't long, but its meaning went far. She bit at her lip as she pulled away, and Thomas lowered his forehead to hers and rested it there.

With her wrapped in his arms in the parking lot of the hospital, Thomas realized he needed to do some mending. He'd warded off love and commitment his entire adult life. He'd promised himself he'd never fall in love, get married and—heaven forbid—he'd never have children. However, with Carissa, he felt different—as though a battle were brewing inside of him that he was afraid he wasn't going to win.

Thomas swiped his hand over his forehead as he headed back outside for another two-by-four from the bed of the truck. For hours, they had measured, cut, and pounded nails into wood. Jeremy and Thomas framed doorways while Carissa and David built the walls that would separate the individual classrooms. He'd mentioned a theory room once more, but the eye roll from Carissa had him zipping his lip and going about his work with Jeremy in silence.

Again, his crisp, white shirt was not holding up to the task of construction. From now on, he thought to himself, he'd pack a bag for spur-of-the-moment manual labor.

David sipped from a bottle of water Carissa had brought back from 7-Eleven. He wiped his brow with his hand and looked around the half-constructed walls of the school.

"When does the electrician come in?" David asked.

"Tuesday."

David nodded, looking around. "I think we're ready for him. He should be done by the end of the week. I fly out on Friday, and I'm back by the following Tuesday. That should give him plenty of time for inspections, and then we can start drywall."

"I think we're making good progress," Jeremy added.

Carissa surveyed the school.

"Tonight we'll sit and brainstorm on how we're going to run. We need to order instruments, music, chairs…"

"Like you said," David interrupted her, "we can talk about that tonight." He kissed the top of her head and followed Jeremy outside to start packing up.

Thomas stepped in closer to Carissa as she continued to gaze around the school.

"Feel better now that you pounded some nails?" He absentmindedly ran his hand down her hair, which she'd secured into a ponytail with the help of a carpenter's pencil.

"Yeah. A run before dinner and I think I'll be ready to move on to the next step." Her eyelashes swept upward as she looked up at him. The soft appearance of a dimple in her cheek sped up his heart rate, and he caught his breath.

Thomas only nodded. He assumed she meant the next step of the planning of the school, but her tone could have been construed as another meaning altogether. He pulled back his hand and tucked it into his pocket.

Again his fingers were itching to play, which meant he was uncomfortable in the situation. He needed to get a grasp on his feelings. Either he was all in, or he needed to get out.

Carissa's run hadn't taken the edge off her attitude as she'd hoped it would. Between the construction at the school, the planning that went into it, and her new co-worker—whom she was having difficulties concentrating around—she felt as though everything was piling in on her.

She'd called Katie only to have her tell her to leave her alone and spend some time getting to know Thomas. That certainly hadn't helped the situation. So she dragged her butt back to the house after only a few miles, showered quickly, and they arrived at Sophia's house promptly at five-thirty, which was mandatory on Sunday evening as far as Sophia was concerned. Family dinner around Sophia's table was every week whether David was in town or not. It would be, however, the first time they didn't have Katie there, and that broke Carissa's heart.

Thomas had insisted on bringing a bottle of wine he'd saved from Italy. It was a celebration of sorts.

"I knew this was one of your favorites." He handed the bottle to Sophia.

"Thomas, this is wonderful. I'll put it in the fridge to get a chill on it." She kissed him on the cheek as Carissa slid past him to find her sister. She saw the extended table set in the living room.

"Oh, looks like we're having a few more for dinner," Carissa commented.

"Mary Alice, Jeremy, and the boys. They'll be along in a bit."

"All the boys?"

"Parker and William are home for the weekend. Elijah thought bringing his three boys would be too much. But we thought this would be fun."

Hope was busy folding napkins and laying them next to each plate. "Grandma showed me how once," she explained. "I thought I'd give it a try."

"Okay, show me." Carissa sat down next to her sister and let her instruct her on the finer art of napkin folding.

Hope explained how to fold each napkin so that it would stand in the center of the plate. Carissa paid attention to every detail, but she was fully aware that when her mother had moved to answer the front door Thomas had stayed, leaning up against the doorjamb and watching them. It sent a surge through her, kicking her heart rate up again.

She was beginning to despise that he could do that to her.

Carissa looked up from the table and met his eyes. "You should learn how to do this."

"C'mon, Thomas, I'll teach you," Hope offered.

"Can't pass that up, can I?" He walked to the table and sat down next to Hope.

Thomas stood as Sophia entered the room carrying the wine he had brought for dinner. Her smile thanked him as she pointed to her guests and gave them a specific seat around the table.

"Thomas has brought us my most favorite wine, straight from Italy."

Thomas quickly stood and reached for the bottle. "Here, let me pour."

Mary Alice took a sip. "Oh, this is wonderful."

"Only the best for Sophia." Thomas felt the sting of David's eyes on him.

Sophia assessed the table as he continued pouring the wine. "You forgot your glass."

"Oh, I'm saving the last drop for you." He topped off Sophia's glass then sat down next to Carissa, who looked up at him with smiling eyes over the rim of her wine glass.

Thomas couldn't remember the last time he'd had a family dinner that included friends. Sure, in Italy eight years ago, the family was Sophia, Pablo, Pierre, Sandra, and himself. They ate together, rehearsed together, traveled together, and often lived communally. However, it was nothing like sitting at the dinner table with the family he was quickly falling in love with, and their dearest friends.

Jeremy leaned back in his chair and patted his stomach when he'd finished his second helping. "Sophia, you absolutely make the best lasagna. I swear I gain three pounds each time I eat it."

David laughed at his friend. "At least she can cook. I just get indigestion when we eat at your house. I mean, seriously, how many years does it take one man to learn to cook a steak?"

"He'll never learn," Parker piped in. "That's why I had to have you teach me."

David lifted his glass of fine Italian wine in a toast. "And that's why my godson loves me best."

Jeremy threw his napkin across the table at David.

David smiled broadly. "I'd say dinner next week should be at your house then, and we'll let Parker cook."

"Can't do it. I'll be in Vegas." Parker raised his eyebrows playfully.

"Vegas? Why?"

"Got a girl. She wants to go." He looked around the table. "Do I have to go on?"

Mary Alice covered her ears with her hands. "Please don't." She shook her head and laughed. Then she turned toward Carissa. "Let's talk about this school of yours. Tell me about it."

"Well…" Carissa wiped her mouth with her napkin and replaced it in her lap. "Dad, Jeremy, and Thomas have all the walls framed. The electrical contractor comes Tuesday, and after inspection, we can drywall. After that, it's flooring, painting, and the finishing touches."

"And students," Sophia added.

"Yes, and students." Carissa's eyes dipped down to her plate.

Mary Alice shifted her arms to rest on the table. "You're worried about that part?"

"Of course I am. I'm worried that I won't have enough students the moment I open the doors. I've done the number crunching, and it scares me. But if I didn't think it was possible, I wouldn't have bought the building."

Thomas shifted in his chair. "I was giving that some thought. You have a few students of your own, and I know your schedule is full for after school. But we have the untapped market of adults, too. And I was thinking, if we moved the piano out of the study, I could start taking on students, too. Two students at one time is better than one. What if parents took piano lessons while their child took cello lessons? There's no reason we should wait to build." He sucked in a breath. "Or maybe you could teach the physical playing, and I can handle the theory."

David gave an approving nod and gestured in his direction, stopping him from the rant he felt coming. "He's got a point."

Sophia began to gather plates. "So, we should do some advertising and get flyers into the schools now."

Carissa smiled as she listened to everyone's excited ideas. "I think it's a good idea to take on multiple students." Her eyes settled on Thomas's, but she hadn't accepted his proposal of theory—yet again.

After dinner, Carissa sat quietly at the table while David, Jeremy, and the boys escaped to the patio for a beer.

She sat with her notebook full of ideas and notes for the and waited for her mother and Mary Alice to join her and Thomas at the table. "We need a detailed list of the instruments we need to purchase. For now, we'll have to keep them in house until we begin to turn a profit, and then we can rent them out long term."

"We need to make sure to talk to the insurance company about that, too. We'll need that in the policy for replacement," Thomas added, and Carissa wrote it down on her list.

"Where are you getting the instruments?" Mary Alice asked.

"I'll have to go to Chicago. I've been working with a dealer there, and he has the best prices for what we need. I plan on going out before Christmas."

Thomas sat forward on the edge of his seat. "What about theory? Do you have a beginning theory book picked out?"

"I have a basic one that will go with my lessons."

"I think theory should be the first thing you teach before they touch anything."

Carissa set her eyes on him and noticed how his jaw had set when he spoke. She'd hoped he'd forget about his damn theory room and teaching it. She did teach theory, but she didn't see the need to cut into student playing time with it. It was part of the hands-on teaching.

Thomas shifted, resting his clasped hands on the table and keeping his stare on her. "Half the problem with students is they start to fool around on the instrument and never learn the music properly. They try to pick out songs by ear, and then you can't go backward and make them do it right. If they aren't sat down and taught what's what first, then the lessons don't mean much."

"But if you don't let them touch the instrument and fall in love with it, theory is useless."

"Fact remains you can't run until you walk. You have to learn how to read music and then touch the instrument."

"It's open for interpretation." Her voice was low and resonated with her irritation.

"Not in my classes." He sat back and folded his arms over his chest. "No finger touches a key until they know how to read the music I'm going to put before them."

Carissa narrowed her eyes on him. Was he really sitting in her mother's house telling her how he was going to run a class? Wasn't he the employee? "You're going to bore them to death first?"

"I don't think theory is boring. Not if it's done properly."

"Well then, you really don't understand young minds, do you?" Carissa, too, sat back in her chair and folded her arms across her chest. He wasn't going to win this argument. It was her school.

Sophia stood. "I think I'll get us some coffee.

Mary Alice followed her.

"Oh, is this our first lover's spat?" Mary Alice's voice had a giddy edge to it.

"Looks that way." Sophia tried to listen as she started the coffee brewing.

The tones from the other room became softer, but more heated. It took straining on a trained ear to catch the conversation, but when Carissa stood with a huff and the front door slammed shut, Sophia knew the argument had finished and neither side had won.

She walked back to the table with a tray of coffee mugs and the coffee pot. "Well, did you get that worked out?" she asked Carissa, who had her head on her arms against the table.

"He's so stubborn!" She flung her hands in the air. "He's got those stupid things in his head and then spins them all around. Every time we're in the damn school, he mentions a theory room. Theory this. Theory that. Dammit, it's my school."

Sophia poured a cup of coffee and set it in front of her daughter.

"Did you at least say you'd consider thinking about it?"

"You're going to side with him?" She shook her head. "This is my school. I'll run things the way I see fit. I can't believe you're just going to side with him."

"I see valid points on both sides."

"Of course you would. Wouldn't want to ruffle the feathers, would you?"

Carissa knew the words she was using were hurtful, though she hadn't meant them to be.

Her mother set down the coffeepot. "Well, I see we're in a nasty mood. I think I'll go sit with the boys out back." She stepped out onto the porch.

Carissa sat at the empty table with only Hope looking up at her. Hope probably had plenty to say to her, too, if she didn't look like Carissa had just crushed her world by fighting with Thomas. She decided it was better to say goodnight and head back home. Besides, it was dark, and she only could assume he knew his way back to the house on foot. God, she'd been an idiot, and her stomach was churning because of it.

She poked her head outside and found her mother, seated on her father's lap, her sad eyes looking back at her. "I'm going to go. Thank you for everything."

Sophia stood and walked toward her.

"I love you." She cupped Carissa's face in her hands and kissed her cheek.

"I know. I'm so sorry."

Sophia pulled her into her arms and held her.

Carissa kissed her sister goodbye and gathered her notebook and purse. Maybe she had been too hard on him, and it would be worth listening to his side—maybe.

Carissa let the door slam behind her has she headed home. Why couldn't it just all work out the way she planned it to? Was she really wrong about her approach?

Chapter Six

Carissa could hear Thomas moving about in his room when she opened the front door. Light gleamed under his bedroom door, but as she climbed up the steps, it blinked out. Deliberately, she supposed.

Well, she couldn't blame him. They'd asked him to move to Kansas City, give up everything else in his life, and then she wouldn't even listen to him when he offered suggestions. They were good suggestions, too. She'd been a fool. Now she cursed herself.

She stood outside his door and thought about knocking, but she refrained. They would talk in the morning when they'd both calmed down. She would hear him out. Theory was a good idea, and it was, of course, included in everything she taught, but she'd never thought of teaching it exclusively as a class. He'd obviously given it a lot of thought, and he was the true professional when she thought about it.

Carissa walked to her room and shut the door.

Thomas leaned his head against the door as he heard her's close. He'd almost flung it open and given her a piece of his mind. Oh, she was stubborn. Then he let out a laugh. Sophia might not have been her biological mother, but they sure as hell made quite a match. The thought washed over him. Stubborn, that might have been too mild for Sophia. What went beyond stubborn? After all, she'd left the man she loved and stayed away for ten years. Not once did she even contact him to hear his side of the story. Well, by God, Carissa was going to listen to his side. If she wanted him to work with her, she was going to listen.

He pulled his shirt off, exchanged his slacks for a pair of sweatpants, and climbed into his bed. He ran his fingers through his hair then laced them behind his head. God, if she was this crazy about her music education, what was going to happen when he took her to bed?

He wanted that more now than he wanted to work side by side with her. No, he needed to get over it. He wasn't the kind of man Carissa needed. She needed stability. She needed a family man. He wasn't that.

He took his pillow and pounded it into place. He closed his eyes.

A smile crossed his lips as he thought of the kiss he and Carissa had shared earlier that morning. She walked up to him out of the darkness and kissed him again. This time, however, the phone didn't ring. Nothing stopped him from touching her, caressing her, and he started to undress her.

The buttons on her blouse released with ease, and her skirt pooled to the ground. She moaned his name and began to undress him.

The room went black. He was alone.

Huddled in the closet, he was no longer a man of thirty-three, but a young man of sixteen. The same closet had found him cowering most of his life.

He twisted, trying to break out of the closet. His face throbbed, his head pounded and his hands…oh, the pain in his hands.

"Sarah!" he called out, but his voice didn't register. "Sarah!" Again and again, he cried out, but there was no sound.

He could hear her scream. He could hear his mother's screams. He could vividly hear his father's shouts, his slaps, his fists on skin, and then there was silence.

Hands were on him. He batted them away.

Carissa was out of breath. She'd run down the hall. She'd tried to force his locked door open. Then she'd gone through the bathroom and to his side. He was twisted in his sheets, pushing at her, flailing his arms about…protecting himself.

"Help her!"

"Thomas, help who? Wake up." She tried to touch him again, but he batted her touch away. "Oh, baby, wake up."

He sat straight up in bed. His eyes flew open. She watched as they settled from terror in his sleep to alertness.

"I'm here. I'm here." She wanted to touch him again, but didn't dare.

His hair was damp from sweat. He held his hands up and looked them over.

Carissa stood. "I'll get you some water." He grabbed her arm and pulled her back.

"No, please don't go."

His hand, damp and hot, trembled against her skin. She covered it with hers. "Are you all right? I heard you screaming from my room."

"What time is it?"

"Three o'clock."

"I'm sorry," he said, catching his breath and moving back from her. "I have nightmares sometimes. I didn't mean to scare you."

"You were hurt. Someone was hurting you." She reached for his face, and he jerked back before he let her hand settle on his cheek.

"Not me. Someone else."

"Oh, Thomas." She pulled him into her arms and held him there. All the anger she'd had for him when she'd thrown herself into her bed was gone. She just wanted to hold him and be there for him.

His breath began to settle as Carissa's hand stroked the back of his neck. Her cheek pressed up against his, and it was soft. Her scent was filling his senses, and he lifted his hands to her arms and ran them softly from her shoulders to her hands until she pulled back slowly.

Their eyes locked. He raised his hand and cupped the back of her neck. Her chest rose in anticipation as he lowered his mouth to hers. He tried to be gentle, tried to take it slow, but he couldn't resist. He parted her lips with his tongue and took. He pulled her closer and felt her respond as he felt his own passion rise.

He pulled her down on top of him. Her body molded to his. His hands slid up her back, gathering her tank top and pulling it over her head. She shook back her head. Her hair fell over her shoulders, over him, like satin on his skin. Thomas looked down between them. Her ripe breasts pressed against his chest. Her heart beat against his.

In a fluid movement, he rolled her onto her back and drank in the beauty that was beneath him. His hand skimmed over her satin skin, cupping her breasts in his hands. Carissa arched her back and closed her eyes. Her body welcomed him.

He lowered his mouth to her neck as she ran her hands over his back.

"Thomas." Her voice was breathless. He pulled back and let himself sink into her eyes. "I want you to make love to me."

There was now nothing more on his mind. He rose and shoved his pants from his legs. He ravaged her shoulders, her neck, and her mouth as he pulled the boxers she'd worn to bed from her body.

It seemed like there wasn't time to explore. Her legs spread under his weight, and he plunged. She arched and rode with him as he rocked into her.

She nipped at his mouth as he whispered her name against her lips. Her heart pounded in her chest. She'd been touched, kissed, and taken over the edge enough to know no one had ever made her feel like he was making her feel. Every muscle in her body quivered as he moved his body over hers—in hers. The racing of her heart, which beat in perfect time with his, only fueled the moment. Never in her life had she wanted a man more than she wanted Thomas.

His eyes met hers as she climbed with him. Their bodies tensed. Every note she'd ever played drummed in her ears as they spilled over together in a crescendo.

He buried his face in her neck. His breath was heavy in her ear as she pulled his shuddering body against her.

When he became still, she held him tighter. She didn't want the moment to end—ever. Greed had taken over. She wanted more of those moments.

Thomas lifted his face to look into hers. He touched her hair and shifted just enough to lessen his weight on her. Carissa watched him as his breath returned to normal. She reached for his hand and laced their fingers together.

"I never want to let go of you." Her eyes were fixed on his and hazy. The words were breathless and sincere. She'd never wanted to hold someone so close to her, always afraid she'd be disappointed in the end. But suddenly it didn't matter, except that his eyes changed and he rolled onto his back.

She turned on her elbow and looked down at him. "And that just scared the hell out of you."

"Maybe this was a mistake."

"We've been at each other since the minute you walked into this house." She rolled up and found the boxers and tank top she'd had on. "The sexual tension was there."

"So that's all this was? Sexual tension?" Now he sounded annoyed, and that had her stewing in confusion.

She yanked the tank top over her head. "What the hell am I supposed to think? Did you or did you not want to sleep with me?"

He clamped his jaw and looked away.

Carissa rose and slid into her boxers. She turned to walk out, but he grabbed her wrist.

"Carissa, don't leave. Stay with me." He rose up as she turned to him. "Sleep in my arms. I was wrong. This wasn't a mistake." He reached his other hand up her arm and pulled her toward the bed. "I want to hold you. I want to wake with you."

Carissa sat on the edge of the bed. She looked into his eyes in the moonlit room. They seemed lost. She put her hand on his cheek and held it there. "What scared you? That wasn't the first time you've had that dream."

He shook it away. "I don't want to talk about it. I just want to be with you right now. I want you in my arms." He ran his hands up her arms to her shoulders and pulled her back down to the bed with him.

"I want to know you, Thomas." She leaned in to kiss him. "I want there to be more between us than just sexual tension."

His lips had lost the softness she'd felt as they'd roamed over her. The sincerity in his eyes had gone dark, and she wondered if he'd ever open up and share his life with her.

The sun was peeking through the curtains. He breathed in her silence as she slept in his arms. He'd made sure they were around her all night long. He didn't want her to escape him. Never had he wanted to hold so tightly to anyone.

She stirred and opened her eyes.

"Good morning." Her lips curled into a sleepy, seductive smile.

"Good morning." He brushed her mouth with a gentle kiss. "I didn't think it was possible for you to be more beautiful than you usually are. I was wrong."

"Thank you." She shifted to get out of bed, but he held her in place.

"Not yet. I want to look at you some more."

"We need to get to the school and clean up before the electrical contractor shows up tomorrow. I also have students, and so do you."

He lifted his head and looked at her with a cocked brow. "I have students?"

"One." She nipped at his lip. "Let's take a shower."

Carissa stood and walked toward the bathroom. He propped up on his elbow and watched her walk away. The very fine tone of her body was only more beautiful now that he had touched and tasted every inch of it. Her sleep-tangled hair swayed down her sculpted back, accentuating the perfect roundness of her bottom, which was barely covered by the boxers she wore. When she turned her head back to him, he smiled.

Her eyes became playful as she pulled the tank top over her head and arms and let it drop to the floor.

He sat up. When she crooked her finger to say come, he flew from the bed and gathered her in his arms. Her laughter filled his ears and his heart. Even as he swept her from her feet, reached into the shower to start the water, and felt her lips on his skin, he knew he'd have to give a little of himself to her to keep her. That's what he wanted. He wanted to keep her. He just wasn't sure he could.

As a man, he could hold his own against other men. As a musician, there wasn't an instrument or piece of music he couldn't master. As a lover, however, he lacked the knowledge of how to care for and love a woman the way he felt Carissa should be cared for and loved.

It amazed Thomas that Carissa could dress and have coffee brewed before he was dressed and ready. Her hair was still wet, and her clothing was casual. He assumed she'd change before her first student, once they returned from the school.

She was staring out the window into the backyard when he walked up behind her and laced his arms around her waist. He settled his hands on her stomach and felt her tighten. "There is something about the morning," she said softly, leaning into him.

"Promise of a new day with new things to come." The scent of her shampoo lingered in the air around her, a clean start to a new day, he thought.

She sighed in agreement. Slowly, she turned in his arms and lifted hers around his neck. "It's been an eventful few days."

"It has. I'm not sure what to think of it."

"Let's do ourselves a favor and not think about it. Let's enjoy it. Let's enjoy each other for as long as we can."

The words, he realized, were spoken by someone who took her days one at a time. When the sun rose, she would start, and when it would set, she would finish. Because of it, there was pain in her eyes—he knew it. He was familiar with how it looked in his own eyes every morning.

"How about I make breakfast? Nothing fancy, but I can fry up an egg and make toast."

"That sounds nice." She touched his cheek and ran her fingers through his hair. "I'm going to go practice. Do you mind?"

"I think that would be a wonderful idea."

Carissa turned to leave the room, and he caught her arm. "Carissa." She turned back to him. "Sleep in my arms again tonight." He lifted his hand to her hair. The damp strands slid beneath his fingers as he stroked his hand down its length. Those long, dark strands gave her a power, he thought. She seemed invincible, and he wished he knew how that felt. "Share my bed from now on."

"Thomas, I need to tell you something." She rubbed her hand across her lips. "I've never…"

"Never?" He raised his eyebrows at her.

She huffed out a laugh. "What I mean is I've never slept with someone mere days after meeting him. I know I told you I wasn't going to take my time, but…"

"Carissa, what happened happened. I don't think any less of you because we moved things along much faster than either of us would have normally."

"So you've never done this? I mean, you've always taken more than four days to know the person you took to bed?" Her eyes opened wide, and he knew the answer she was fishing for. He'd have liked to have more time before he had the chance to even put a crack in her heart, much less before breaking it completely. But he wasn't going to lie to her.

Thomas diverted his eyes and stood up taller.

Carissa stepped back from him. "I guess not."

"Carissa, I won't lie to you. That's not the way I like to start a relationship either." Her eyes opened even wider when he said relationship. "Pablo was—is—a very popular man. He's sexy and talented and comes across as the perfect citizen of the world. Women and men want him."

"That's Pablo. Tell me what that has to do with Thomas."

He took a moment then looked her in the eye. "There are…leftovers." He hated how he said it the moment it came out.

"Leftovers?"

"What I mean is…"

"I know what you mean. You slept with those who couldn't get to the top."

"Carissa, I was young. I wasn't looking—"

"Stop." She held her hand up between them. "We're not married. We're not even together really." He shifted uncomfortably. "If that's who you are…"

"It's not." He reached for her. He felt her stiffen beneath his touch. "I don't use people for sex or advancement. Maybe, in the past," he admitted to her and himself, "I did indulge when a woman wanted to share the evening with me, but I didn't actively seek out women to use."

"But they were there."

"Dammit, Carissa. I'm trying to open up to you." He stepped away from her and walked around the kitchen. "I'm not that kind of person. Usually, well-to-do women came on to me, and I was young and impressionable. I did it. I'm being honest with you."

Carissa nodded. There were tears in her eyes, and the silence between them was deafening. He hated that everything about him was bound to drive her away.

"I am telling you this now so you'll understand." He walked back to her and wrapped his hands around her arms. "I have never slept in the same bed with a lover before. I've never awoken to see someone there next to me. I have never held anyone else like I held you last night."

He watched her process what he had told her.

"Go practice." He kissed her on the forehead. "I'll make breakfast for us." He forced a smile toward her, and she returned one equally as forced.

Carissa shut the door to the study and leaned against it. She was in over her head now. She never should have gotten into bed with him.

She batted back the tears that wanted to fall. She believed him, even though she didn't want to. At that moment, it would be easier to just walk away and pretend none of it meant anything. But that would be a lie.

Oh, who was she kidding? She had wanted to sleep with him since the moment their eyes locked that first time.

She took out her cello and arranged herself in the chair. She closed her eyes and began to play and drown the world and its truths away for a while.

When she emerged from the study, she could smell breakfast, but he hadn't come to get her. She felt the anger brewing in her belly again.

He'd probably left, just like he had when they'd fought at her parents' house. He wasn't up to the battle—or the confrontation. It would be his loss. She wasn't stewing anymore. She could handle what he had to say now. Wasn't it just like him to… When she turned the corner into the kitchen, her mother was sitting with Thomas at the table. Each held a mug of coffee with one hand, and their other hands grasped together in the center of the table. Smiles permeated their lips. They were so comfortable together. Wouldn't that be nice? To fall in love with a man her mother was so fond of.

She shook the thought from her head. Fall in love—that wasn't even an option at the moment.

Thomas gazed up at her. "That was beautiful."

"Thank you. I thought you were going to come get me." She moved toward the coffeepot and poured a cup.

"I was too busy listening." His eyes were soft, like they'd been when she'd lain in his arms.

Sophia laughed. "He was so busy listening to you, he burned breakfast."

Thomas shrugged. "Sophia saved me." He lifted his coffee mug to toast her.

"I'll make you some breakfast." She stood and began to busy herself making breakfast for Carissa. "I was talking to Principal Parsons the other day. They've just replaced the piano in the school, and I asked him if there was anything wrong with the other. His answer was, "Mrs. Murphy." She looked over at Thomas. "She's the music teacher, and she's horrible. But he said he'd sell us the piano for a good price."

Carissa's mouth gaped open. "Mom, that would be great. I was afraid we'd have to take the one from the study."

"No. That's Millie's, and it stays here." Sophia added sternly, and Carissa nodded.

"I'd be happy to have a look at it if you'd like." Thomas offered.

Sophia set the eggs on the counter. "I think that would be wonderful." She cracked an egg into the skillet and let it sizzle a moment before cracking another. "Thomas, I was thinking it would be really nice if you could go with Carissa to Chicago, too."

Carissa watched him think about the proposition too hard. He bit his lip, and his eyes shifted to his coffee. The anger from before reappeared, and she set her jaw.

"Really, if there's a problem…"

"No." He looked up at her. "No problem." He lifted his mug to his lips, but it didn't hide his eyes. Carissa knew

Chicago had something to do with the nightmare he'd had last night.

Whatever had happened to Thomas, it had happened in Chicago.

Carissa backed the car out of the driveway and started down the street toward the school.

Thomas adjusted in his seat and turned toward her.

"Does your mother come around like that often?"

With a smile, Carissa nodded. "Yes, on Monday mornings she usually stops by and has coffee with Katie and me." The words began to catch in her throat when she realized Katie hadn't been there to be part of it this morning.

Thomas laid his hand on hers as it rested on the gearshift.

"She's going to be okay."

"I know." She sniffed back her tears. "It's just not the same without her in the house. My whole life has been taking care of her and Millie."

The tears weren't stopping. She pulled the car to the side of the road with a jerking stop.

Thomas lifted her hand to his lips and gave it a gentle kiss. "Why did you choose that?"

"What?" She wiped at her eyes.

"Why would a young woman choose to stay and take care of two elderly women instead of auditioning for the symphony, or touring, or recording?"

"You sound like you're accusing me." Though she wasn't sure of what exactly.

"Well, maybe I am. Why didn't you do more with your life?"

"I do plenty with my life." The tears were beginning to dry up, and anger was beginning to stir in her.

"What have you done?"

"Who are you to ask me?"

"I'm the man whose arms you woke up in this morning," he said as if she needed reminding.

She gasped. Was that enough to make demands on her? He seemed to think so. "I'll have you know I went to college."

"Okay, where did you live when you went to college?" He'd crossed his arms over his chest, and the smug look on his face pissed her off.

"I went to Missouri State."

"That wasn't my question. Where did you live, Carissa?"

"What does it matter?"

"It's the question at hand."

"Fine. I lived on campus for one semester then I lived with Millie and Katie."

His lips thinned into a smile, and she felt hers tighten. "Why are you looking at me like that?"

"You are afraid of moving on." His smile widened.

"Go to hell, Thomas."

"Whatever, but you are so afraid of letting go of what you have here that it's only held you back."

"You don't know what the hell you're talking about!" She shifted in her seat, checked her mirrors, and shifted the car into drive.

"Oh, I know plenty." He leaned back against the seat, his arms still crossed over his chest.

He'd run away when it had all gotten too hard for him. She, on the other hand, chose the comforts of home, and it had probably cost her what could have been a very nice career as a professional musician. He didn't belittle what she did. Teaching others music was wonderful, and he, himself, would be doing that same thing come four o'clock. But he'd been a professional musician playing to sold-out crowds, and he knew talent. Carissa Kendal had more talent than most of the performers he knew. He'd almost venture to say she rivaled Sophia and, with the right venue, would surpass her.

There wasn't another word until they stopped in front of the school. Carissa took the keys from the ignition and turned to him. "What about this?" She pointed out the window. "What about the school? Do you think that's doing nothing?"

"No."

"After all, big, professional musician, where are you working? Why did you move halfway across the world to come here and work?"

"I've made a name for myself, Carissa."

"Sure, then why aren't you in Europe now?" She watched him shift his gaze out the window, and his tongue skimmed over his teeth. He was uncomfortable talking about it. It was painfully obvious. "There's something there. Don't sit here and accuse me when you have a secret you're holding on to."

"Why do you think that?" He turned his head back to her with a snap.

"You wouldn't talk about your dream. You haven't told me why you were so anxious to move back to the States and give up all that professionalism. And this morning when my mother mentioned you going to Chicago with me, I thought you were going to run."

"Well, you've done a lot of observation in the past few days too, haven't you?"

"You said you wanted to get to know me. I guess I want to get to know you, too."

"Fair enough." He let the air simmer between them. "Let's take it one day at a time. You give me a little, and I'll give you a little." Which was a lot, he decided.

How long could he remain in her good graces before she kicked him to the curb when she found out about his father, his sister, and his nearly killing Pierre?

Chapter Seven

The drive home from visiting Katie at the hospital was silent. Katie hadn't been too talkative, and Thomas knew that Katie's weakened state was wearing on Carissa. Katie was nervous about moving into an assisted living home, though she thought by being so damn pleasant about it all she wasn't letting on. Katie wasn't the only one pretending. He'd spent almost twenty minutes alone with Katie when Carissa had gone to find the restroom, and when Carissa returned, Thomas was sure she'd been crying.

Carissa laid her purse by the stairs when they walked through the front door of the house. "I'm going to take a shower. My first student will be here at three thirty and yours at three forty-five." She sucked in a ragged breath and rubbed her eyes, tired and red from the crying she'd eminently denied. "I can teach in the living room, and you can use the study. Tomorrow we'll move the piano."

She turned and walked up the stairs, leaving him alone watching her disappear down the hall. Sophia had said Carissa was afraid of losing people. Millie had died, and that had done its part of scaring her away from doing more adventurous things than teaching out of the study of her house. He knew what it was like to lose someone so important to you. If he could only tap into his own feelings, he could share with her what he knew of living for the moment and then moving on. But that was the coward in him that had him running to Italy in the first place. He'd never dealt with the loss of his sister, or his family. How could he help prepare Carissa and give her any kind of emotional support when he couldn't even face talking about his family?

By three fifteen, Carissa had moved her few items into the living room to begin her lesson. Thomas walked into the room with a bouquet of daises in his hands, and a smile crossed her lips when she saw him. "Mr. Samuel, what are you doing?"

"Well, Ms. Kendal, it appeared to me that you could use a little pick-me-up. My mother always liked daises for that." He moved toward her and she stood, taking the daises in her arms.

"They're beautiful, Thomas." She shifted her eyes to his.

He brought his hand to her cheek and caressed it gently. "You deserve to always be happy."

She wanted to speak. She wanted to say something witty and charming, but all of her words were stuck behind the lump in her throat and the tears that were stinging her eyes.

He lingered his gaze and then shifted it to the window.

"Well, I see your student just pulled up. Let me put those in water, and they'll be waiting for you."

"Thank you, Thomas." Her words finally found their way out.

He stared out of the room and then turned back to her. "Oh, I wanted to ask, does this student of mine have any playing experience?"

She tucked her lips between her teeth to keep her smile from taking over. "She just chose her instrument, but she does have a lot of theory under her belt. That should please you." He smiled with a nod. "I think you'll be amazed at what she knows when she gets here."

He nodded and disappeared into the kitchen.

Thomas made quick work of the lesson plans that Carissa kept for the piano. He knew where he would start, and he knew just how to proceed. He could hear the sharp and flat notes of a whining violin from the other room. Normally the sound would've made him wince. But knowing Carissa was just out of view, sharing her love of music with a child, gave the unmelodious tones a poignancy that made him smile.

He heard tapping at the door and hurried to answer it before it disrupted Carissa and her young student.

A little face, framed in blonde hair, smiled up at him. He chuckled. "Miss Hope Kendal, are you my student?"

"Yep. Mom let me choose the piano as my instrument," she said, holding Sophia's hand and absolutely beaming.

"Okay, then, go wash your hands and dry them well. Then meet me in the study," he instructed.

"Wash my hands?" She was on her way to the bathroom as she looked back at him.

"You never touch a beautiful piano with dirty hands." He watched Sophia turn to compose herself as she coughed back a laugh.

"Thank you, Thomas. I don't know why she changed her mind. She kept telling me she was going to play the cello too, but then you arrived and now it's the piano."

"She might change her mind again," he assured her in a whisper as he closed the door.

"If you don't mind, I'll stay during her lesson, but in Katie's room. I need to pack up some of her things to take to the center so she feels more at home."

He touched her arm gently. "I think that would mean a lot to her."

Hope bounded back down the hall. "Okay, I'm ready." She flexed her fingers, causing Thomas to laugh as he laid a finger to his lips to remind her to be quiet while Carissa was teaching.

Hope nodded. "Are you staying, Mom?" she whispered.

"I'll be in Katie's room. I know the rules. No parents allowed."

She gave them a wave and walked toward the kitchen to get a glass of water before diving into her grandmother's things.

When Sophia walked into the kitchen, she saw the daisies and smiled. He was falling in love with her daughter. She could feel it. Warmth spread through her. She'd known when she'd called him that it was the right choice. Thomas Samuel would never hurt someone he loved. He'd fight every battle to keep her safe and happy. Carissa still needed that. She needed someone to make her feel welcome, wanted, and loved. She'd been hopeful that someone would be Thomas.

Sophia filled her glass and sipped slowly. Even after all the years she'd been blessed to be Carissa's mother, she knew her daughter still strived to keep hold of everything and everyone she held dear. Sophia shook her head, thinking about what the first seven years of her life must have been like while Mandy, Carissa's mother, still had custody of her. She was in and out of strangers' houses while her mother was stoned and passed out somewhere. To not know where your mother was half the time and to have her lie to you about your own father was unconceivable to Sophia.

It hadn't been easy to win Carissa's love. She was a threat to Carissa and always had been. There were so many times she'd wished she'd stayed and asked questions, but her damn pride had kept her away for ten years—missing the man she loved and losing out on Carissa's childhood.

But, she decided, had she not run, she'd never have met Thomas. And it seemed to be Thomas who might actually capture her daughter's heart. Thomas who might make her realize that love is strong, and with it, she would never have to be alone again.

The first faint notes from the study snapped her from her daze. Hope was making music.

Thomas was impressed with Hope's musical knowledge. She knew her bass clef from her treble clef. She knew the notes of the scales. She was familiar with a half note, whole note, and even knew what a rest was. She could put her fingers in the right place at middle C and even humored him with her rendition of "Hot Crossed Buns." In half an hour, she'd flown through what would have been a beginner's first four lessons. However, he could see he'd have his work cut out for him with Hope.

She couldn't stay focused, and she kept looking up from the keys to him and not the music. When he'd catch her doing it, her cheeks would turn red and she'd turn back to the keys and notes.

"Well, Hope, I'm very impressed," he complimented when his timer chimed, indicating their lesson was over.

"I'm going to be as good as you," she said with optimism.

"Thank you. And yes, I think you will." He marked her lesson sheet and handed her a worksheet. "Here is your theory lesson for the week. Bring this back and..." His eyes went wide. Then what?

"Then you'll give me a sticker."

"I will?"

"Uh-huh. Carissa gives you stickers on your paper, and when you get ten stickers, you get to choose a toy from the chest." She pointed to a small cardboard treasure chest in the corner.

He was sure the trinkets inside were the kind that a mother would probably throw away the moment the child wasn't looking, but he also knew they'd play their hearts out to get one of those silly little trinkets. "Okay, then. You do your assignment, and I'll give you a sticker next week."

Hope was satisfied. She jumped up from the bench and headed for the door. She turned back around and hugged Thomas and smiled as her mother walked down the hall toward them. "That was fun."

"I guess she didn't beat you down too much."

Thomas put his arm around Sophia's shoulders and walked them out to the front porch. "I seem to have survived."

The air had cooled considerably and it nipped at him, but the bright ray of light that was Hope Kendal still beamed as she ran through the yard.

Sophia turned to him.

"The flowers you gave Carissa were beautiful. I saw them in the kitchen."

"Oh, yeah, I thought she could use them. She was worked up about Katie, though she wouldn't say so."

Sophia nodded. "She's afraid of being alone."

Thomas turned his eyes to her. "She has her family. She's very lucky." He knew what he spoke of. Family was so important, and he realized that even more now that he was surrounded by one.

"Yes, but she didn't always have her family." She took a deep breath and hollered for Hope to climb into the car. "Thank you, Thomas." She held her hand out for him to shake.

He shook it professionally then pulled her into a hug. "It was my pleasure."

He watched them drive away then turned to head back inside.

"It's not professional to make out with the students' mothers on the front porch." Carissa was in the doorway with her arms crossed over her chest and a smirk on her lips.

Thomas wrapped his arms around her waist and tugged her to him. "What about making out with the teacher on the porch?"

"I have ten minutes till my next student." She reached for his lapel. "I haven't thanked you for the flowers yet." Her eyelashes fluttered up at him.

"Ten minutes isn't enough time to thank me properly," he said as she pulled him through the front door and shut it behind her.

"No, but there's enough time for this." She lifted herself up on her toes and covered his mouth with hers.

The warmth overtook him and sank into his gut. His hand cupped her neck. He slid the other down her back, and a moan escaped her lips. His heart beat harder.

"Thank you for the flowers." Her forehead pressed to his.

"I'll buy you more tomorrow if this is the thank-you."

She let her eyes wander up to his again. "Oh, this was just the promise that I would thank you properly." The smile on her lips was as seductive as the suggestion.

"I could definitely get used to this." The doorbell rang, and Thomas sighed.

"You might want to withhold your judgment for a few minutes." She nipped his nose with a kiss, fixed her blouse, straightened her skirt, and opened the door.

"Clair! How very nice to see you this afternoon." Carissa stood aside as a chubby, little, blonde girl managed to maneuver herself and a cello case through the door. Her cheeks were cherry red, and her pigtails pulled her skin tight, adding to her downright miserable look.

Thomas snuck through the kitchen door as he heard the little girl begin to tell Carissa how much she hated cello lessons.

It was past six when Carissa's last student left. She hadn't seen Thomas in hours, but she knew he was in the next room. The thought comforted her as she finished putting away her music and lesson cards then wiped down her cello. She felt him. When she turned around, he was standing in the doorway.

He'd leaned up against the doorjamb, his thumbs tucked into the pockets of his loose jeans. He had on a crisp, white T-shirt that fit snug to his body, and she bit her lip remembering what was under it. He was barefoot and his hair was tousled, no doubt from his long fingers having been raked through it many times. He was at home, she thought.

He gave her a long, slow smile. "Are you all done?"

"Yes, last student just left." She walked toward him.

"You've had six calls while you were working."

"I have?" She stood before him and lifted her hand to his chest. He didn't shift. He let her touch him and looked straight into her eyes.

"Six new families who are interested in starting lessons before your school opens its doors."

"I'll give them all a call later." She kept her voice calm, but excitement was bubbling over inside her.

"I told them you were with students all afternoon, but would be happy to give them a call back in the morning." He picked up a strand of her hair. "Perhaps you should fill me in on enrollment procedures so I could help them."

"I should do that."

His face was more intriguing than a new piece of sheet music. His jaw showed a shadow of whiskers, and she longed to rub her face against his cheek. His lips were pale in the shadows of the evening, a pleasant contrast to his blue eyes.

Her attention diverted to other things in the house. "What is that smell?"

"Your dinner."

"My dinner?" She shifted her eyes back to his.

Thomas nodded, finally standing up straight and burying his fingers in her hair. "I have one meal I know how to cook well." He let his hands slide over her shoulders and down her arms until their fingers interlocked. "C'mon, darling," he teased, tugging her down the hall.

Candles flickered in the center of the table set for two. There were two wineglasses, hers filled with wine and his filled with ice water. He guided her to her chair and pulled it out for her. She smiled warmly. "Thank you, sir."

"You're most welcome."

Thomas dished out spaghetti and meatballs, and Carissa laughed. "Is this your special meal?"

"Yes." He sat down next to her. "In all my years in Italy, this is what I became good at."

"Oh, you're good at so many things," she said, leaning on the table and looking at him seductively.

"Would you like to embellish on that?"

She moistened her lips with her tongue. "Words will never do it justice."

"Our dinner is going to get cold." He inched toward her.

"We can warm it up later." She ran her hand up his arm and felt him quiver.

Thomas stood and pulled her to her feet so quickly that she fell against him. Taking advantage of the close proximity, she nibbled his throat. He groaned and towed her through the house and up the stairs with her following in laughter.

"I would have taken you in the kitchen, but it still seems to be public domain," he said, leading her through the hallway. "Your bed this time." He pushed open her bedroom door.

Carissa caught the door behind her and gave it a shove before they tumbled onto the bed. Before she caught her breath, Thomas moved his body atop hers and covered her mouth with his, smoldering her senses. Everything she felt, tasted, wanted, and saw was him. He pushed up her skirt, and she surrendered to him. A moment later, she felt him inside her. There was no calm control from him. He was taking her, and she was letting him.

He moved against her in a hunger that surprised even him. He wanted her. He wanted her fast. He wanted all of her.

He took. Her panting breaths and her muffled moans of passion fueled him. Every taste, every sound, every movement breathed another beat of life into him.

Carissa's body molded beneath his, around his, until he was sure they were one entity.

Her skin grew damp under his lips, and her fingernails raked up his skin beneath his shirt. They moved in a symphonic rhythm until the pounding of his heart filled his entire body, and he released as she pulled him to her tighter. Together their bodies became limp, still molded to one another.

He let his body rest against hers. Feeling her heart race beneath his.

"God, you drive me mad," he whispered against her neck.

She lifted her hand to his hair and ran her fingers through it. Her breath was easing. "Thomas?"

"Hmmm?"

"Don't leave me."

He heard her words and took a moment to contemplate them. He shifted his weight off her and rested beside her.

"Where do you think I'm going?"

She shrugged. "I like you. I really like you." She adjusted her skirt to cover her legs. "I'd like to think this isn't a fling."

"Fling?"

"Yeah." She raised herself onto her elbow to meet his eyes. "I don't want to be just one of your women, Thomas. I want to be your woman."

He touched her face and gave thought to what he would say. "I don't come from the kind of family that's good at relationships. I haven't spoken to my mother in sixteen years."

She bit down on her lip, and her eyebrows drew together. "What is that supposed to mean? You won't consider an us?"

"Us? Is that what you think you want, Carissa?" What had he expected? She wasn't the kind of woman who stood by the back door and waited for him to share her bed. She was the kind of woman you waited to take to bed and kept her there forever. It was a vile and disgusting thought that he'd even had that prior kind of experience, and it made it even more poignant that he get that across to her. "You don't know me very well."

Carissa sat up and fisted her hands in her lap. "Thomas, I wouldn't give myself to you like this if I didn't want more. I'm not some easy ride."

"I didn't say you were." He sat up next to her and reached for his discarded pants, pulling them on. "I want you to know I've never been around love like you have."

"Well, let me tell you, the love I've been around has been amazing." She looked up into his eyes. "And I was seventeen before I ever saw it. For a long time, I didn't imagine it could even exist."

He reached for her hand and interlaced their fingers. "Didn't your birth mother and father…"

"What, love each other?"

"Well, yeah." He shrugged, realizing he didn't know anything about her parents really, except what Sophia had shared with him over the years. Then again, she had run away without knowing the entire story. So all he knew was the man Sophia loved had a daughter, and her mother…whatever that had meant.

Carissa laughed. "Oh, that was purely sex."

"Oh." He didn't see David as that kind a man.

"I don't mean when I was young. I mean when I was conceived."

He nodded. "They were young?"

"My mother was. She was seventeen when she got pregnant with me. She'd lied to my dad about her age. They had a quick affair. She got pregnant."

"Wasn't your mother around most of your life?"

"Ten years." She huffed out a breath and shook her head. "Ten miserable years."

He watched as her forehead creased, and she drew her brows together. He imagined it was how he looked to those who asked him about his father.

"You don't sound like you have very many fond memories of her."

"Well..." She took a deep breath. "You're right. I don't. The only decent thing she ever did was give us Hope."

That statement confused him, but she was continuing without giving him an opportunity to clarify. "I want what my dad and Sophia have. I want that kind of relationship. I want that kind of love."

"I've never seen love like that," he admitted. "I'm not sure I've ever believed in it."

"I guess we're back to what I said earlier." She turned to him, their fingers still interlaced. "Please don't leave me."

He thought about what Sophia had said to him about Carissa having a fear of people leaving. He didn't really know what to say to her. He was a runner. He'd run from his past and what he'd started to become. How long could he really stay in her arms before he got scared and ran again? He didn't want to leave her, but he couldn't promise her forever. He was, after all, his father's child. The child of a man who hated, lied, abused, and killed.

He could feel the heat rise in his cheeks, the sweat bead on the back of his neck, and his heart quicken its pace. He was glad the room was growing darker around them. If she could see his eyes clearly, she'd know the truth.

"I won't leave you, Carissa." He tried to keep his voice even, but he was sure he'd just lied.

Carissa woke many times during the night just to check that Thomas was still next to her. He'd said he wouldn't leave her, but she'd heard the quiver in his voice. She still didn't know the man she was falling in love with. The man whose arms she now slept in. But she wanted to, so desperately wanted to, know him.

She'd felt a shift in the air during the night. Snow was coming and so was Halloween, as Hope had already reminded her. In no time at all, construction on the school would be finished, Thanksgiving would be upon them, and the holidays would settle in. Would Thomas still be there?

He stirred in his sleep. The wrinkle between his eyebrows deepened as he slept like a child with his hands folded beneath his cheek. His blond hair was tousled, and his leg peeked out from under the sheet. A smile crossed Carissa's lips. She was so in love with the man, her heart was pounding just from watching him sleep. She bit down on her bottom lip to keep it from quivering. How was she going to make him fall in love with her if he couldn't even promise not to leave and mean it?

By the time Thomas made it down the stairs, the pot of coffee was cold, the scent of toast lingered in the air, and a note waited for him on the table. She'd taken a run to the school to let in the contractor and to drop off more flyers at the grocery store and elementary school. He laughed aloud at the postscript: "Please get the car and meet me at The Spot. I'll need a ride home." He ran back to her room, pulled on his jeans and T-shirt, and found his shoes in his own room. He hurried down the stairs, pulled the keys from the drawer, and headed out the back of the house. Just as quickly, he retreated to his room for a coat. Was she crazy? It was getting much too cold out to be running miles and miles through town.

When he pulled into the parking lot, he could see into the small diner. The breakfast crowd had cleared out, but there was no sign of Carissa inside. He stayed in the car and waited. Ten minutes later, he heard pounding on the trunk of the car. He jumped in his seat, hitting his head on the window.

Carissa was smiling at him as she pulled the door open. "It's warmer inside."

"I was just debating on whether to go looking for you. It's freezing out here." He stepped from the car and pulled his coat tighter as Carissa adjusted the ponytail at the top of her head.

Her breath misted in the cold air, and the chill of her skin warmed as she looked at him. He'd come for her. It was something, she decided. He hadn't left when she wasn't there to wake with him. She stepped in and kissed him lightly.

"Good morning, darling," she said playfully.

"Good morning, dear." His voice joined in the playfulness.

They collected menus as they walked past Betsy with a wave and huddled into the booth in the back corner. He didn't sit across from her. Instead, he pushed her over on the seat and sat down next to her. She turned her face to him. She fretted a moment. Was she feeling false hope? He had said he'd stay. Would he? Could he?

Betsy hobbled to the table. She wore her age and weight like a badge of honor. "You already up and runnin' through town?"

"Will you tell her it's too cold for it, too?" Thomas chimed in.

"I knew I liked your new beau." Betsy winked. "I'll get you both some coffee. You need to warm up," she said to Carissa. "And, honey, you need to wake up." She gave a nod to Thomas.

"She likes you." Carissa nudged him, and he smiled down at her. And I love you, she wanted to say, but didn't dare even take the breath for it.

Thomas looked over the menu. "Everything on here looks so good. I guess I've been away from American food so long I want it all." He looked over at her. "What are you having?"

"I think I'm just going to have a cinnamon roll and some coffee."

"Not me. I'm having ham and eggs, over easy," he added with a nod. "Toast with strawberry jelly and home fries."

"They come with cheese, if you want."

"I want." He closed the menu and playfully raised his eyebrows at her suggestively, and she laughed.

He took her hand in his and gently kissed her fingers. Mornings with Thomas were something she could get very used to. A routine with a man. His things by her sink— their sink, she corrected. A morning full of making coffee and toast for each other and someday getting little ones ready for days at school. Nighttime would come with its own routines of brushing teeth, reading stories, and tucking those same little ones into bed.

Betsy returned with coffee, took their orders, and hurried away toward the counter.

Carissa realized she'd been daydreaming about things she shouldn't be thinking of. She took a sip of coffee to clear her mind. "I got a call from the store in Chicago this morning."

"Hmm," he muttered as he lifted the steaming coffee to his lips.

"I scheduled a meeting with them for November second."

Thomas jerked, splashing coffee down the front of him.

Carissa jumped back and reached for napkins from the dispenser.

"God, are you okay?" She handed him the wad of napkins and went to work helping him dry his clothes. "Did you burn yourself?"

"I'm fine." He snatched the napkins from her hand.

She watched him dab the coffee from his ruined white T-shirt as he muttered curses under his breath. His blue eyes seemed to have clouded.

She sat back away from him. "Are you sure you're okay?"

"I said I was fine." He wadded up the napkins and set them to the side, but when he lifted his mug, she noticed his hands were unsteady.

She was sure Chicago held a secret for Thomas Samuel. Before November second, she'd know what it was.

Chapter Eight

Thomas fumbled through the rest of his day. Acting stupid like he had, spilling his coffee and getting so upset, hadn't set the pace to be much company for the day.

He practiced at the piano for three hours after helping Carissa move it into the living room, and then he took a long, hot shower. He watched some stupid movie while Carissa gave lessons and he tried like hell to recompose himself, but he just couldn't get control over his emotions.

Now he sat in Carissa's bed. His head pounded, his throat was sore, and his hair was damp from sweat. His hands, gripping his head, were shaking.

Carissa stood at the lighted doorway of the bathroom, holding a glass of water.

"Are you okay?" She moved back toward the bed. She looked fresh from sleep, and Thomas looked at the clock on her nightstand. It was just past three in the morning.

He nodded.

She handed him the glass of water and stood back a step. Her eyebrows knit together, and she chewed her lower lip. "Who is Sarah?" she finally asked as he sipped the water she'd brought to him.

He didn't need to ask why she was standing back from him, asking such a question. He'd been dreaming again. It was still as vivid in his head as the pounding of his pulse.

Her hurt expression prodded his conscience. He'd been sleeping in her bed, building a business with her, and letting his heart go to her. It was time he did a little talking.

He finished the glass of water and set it on the nightstand. He adjusted the pillows against the headboard and sat up against them, then reached for Carissa's hand

and pulled her down to the bed so that they sat facing each other.

"Sarah?" he whispered, and she nodded. With a breath of courage, he gave some thought to how much he was about to tell her. "Sarah was my sister."

"Your sister?" He nodded again. "Was?"

He held tight to her hands, and his quivering eased. "She died when she was twelve, on the second of November."

"Oh, Thomas." Her hand shifted to his cheek as her eyes softened. "I'm so sorry. I didn't know—the date." She shook her head, and he knew she'd realized it was the date that had set him off at the diner. She'd be traveling to Chicago on the very date his sister's life had been taken. "I'm sorry. How old were you?"

"Sixteen." The night replayed in his mind over and over. He could hear Sarah, and he had to wait until he stopped hearing her to let the pain in his heart abate before he could finish his story.

Carissa brushed away a tear that had fallen from her eye. "Was she in an accident?"

Dear God, she was trying to walk him through it. He kissed her fingers tenderly as though to appreciate the softness she exuded. What he had to tell her wasn't soft and couldn't be coated to be delivered gently. It was harsh and painful, and she couldn't help him through it. He had to dig deep inside and pull it out the way he remembered it.

"No. It wasn't an accident." He tried to steady himself. "She was killed."

Her gasp ripped through his heart. She covered her mouth, and her eyes filled with tears.

Telling the woman he was falling in love with that his sister was killed—murdered—wasn't as horrible as the rest of the story. Wasn't as horrible as the reason he couldn't fall in love with her. He dreaded the moment when that would come up.

"You said she wasn't in an accident."

He shook his head. "No. It wasn't an accident. Not like you'd think." He shifted uncomfortably. He had to tell her the truth as he knew it. "She was murdered."

Sobbing, Carissa pulled him into her arms. "Oh, Thomas, that's terrible. So terrible." She pulled back to look at him. "How did you find out? Was she near home? Oh, your parents…" Her hand was back over her mouth. "How did you find out?"

He took deep breath and swallowed hard. "I was there."

"You were there? Oh, God!"

His stomach churned at the memory of the horror. "Carissa, I really don't want to talk about this."

"You have to. You have nightmares about this. This is the second time in a week you've woken up screaming her name."

"Third," he admitted. "The nightmares started again the night Katie fell."

"You tried to help her, didn't you? In your dreams, you're trying to find her."

Shamefully, he shook his head. He took his own hands from hers and clenched them together, remembering the pain he'd been in that night. "I was hiding."

She tucked her feet beneath her and moved closer to him. "You have to tell me what happened. Did someone break into your house? I need to know what you've been through."

Thomas shook his head. Having to go back through it all and relay it to another person made him feel young and weak all over again. "I'm afraid."

"Afraid? Afraid of what? You've already been through this."

"No." He gathered her into his arms and buried his face in her hair. He breathed in every detail of her from the scent of her hair to the shape of her body. He wanted to take it all with him when he was forced to leave. "I'm afraid of telling you and what you'll think."

She pulled back and looked him in the eyes. "I may have known you only a little over a week, but I know one thing."

"What is that?"

"I know I've fallen in love with you."

His eyes grew wide, and his already pounding heart beat harder. "Carissa…"

"Don't tell me I shouldn't have said that. I've already told you I watched two people miss a decade of loving each other because they were stubborn. If I get my heart broken, then I'll have to deal with that. I asked you not to leave me, and no matter what you tell me, I'm not getting up and walking out on you."

"But I'm not who you think I am." He saw it flash in her eyes. Fear.

"Thomas, did you kill your sister?"

"No," he answered, and she let out a breath. "It wasn't me that killed her. It was our father."

Tears fell from her eyes, and her breath had stopped for a moment longer than it should have. He could see the shock in her eyes and the paralysis of her body. It was as if he'd hit her with his own hands. He kicked his way from the sheets and climbed out of the bed. He walked to the window and stared down at the empty street.

"You don't want to love someone like me."

"Too late." She walked up behind him and wrapped her arms around him, resting her head against his back. "I do love you. Now, I'm going downstairs and I'm going to start us a pot of coffee. You are going to gather your strength and come down and tell me all about this." She turned him toward her. "I want to know."

"You're going to change your mind." He knew what he'd told her already had shaken her.

"Didn't you promise me not to leave?" Yeah, and he'd said it knowing he'd have to leave when he told her what he'd just told her. What he hadn't yet told her. "Then I'm not going to change my mind." She kissed him softly and left the room. She was wrong. She didn't know.

Thomas let out a sigh of relief when he saw Carissa at the kitchen table in her tank top, boxer shorts, and a blanket wrapped around her, waiting for him. He hadn't scared her away yet.

He took a moment to study her. She was beautiful. She deserved better than him.

The October air had chilled the house. She looked up over her coffee mug at him, and he watched as she let her eyes settle into his. He had to tell her the rest—she was waiting.

It had taken him a half hour to work up the courage to make it down the stairs. Now dressed in a pair of flannel pants and a T-shirt, he shuffled into the kitchen.

She stood to pour him a cup of coffee. "I thought you gave up." She pulled down a mug, filled it, and handed it to him. "C'mon. We're going out to the couch and cuddle and talk."

She was amazing, he thought as he followed her to the living room with his cup of coffee in his hand. It had saddened her and shocked her to learn the bare bones of what had happened. Perhaps, just perhaps, she was going to be able to deal with the details of that horrible night and who he'd become.

Carissa turned on the small lamp on the end table and situated herself on the couch with her legs tucked up under her. She set her coffee on the table and patted the cushion for him to join her. He slowly walked to the couch and sat down. She draped the blanket over both of them, picked up her coffee, and focused her eyes on Thomas. "Now, tell me about what happened."

His mouth had gone dry, and the coffee did nothing to help the matter. His hands still shook so he leaned across her to set his mug on the table. He felt her breath in his ear and the pounding of her heart as his body brushed against hers. As he pulled back, he stopped and laid a gentle kiss on her lips. "That's for taking this much time with me."

"I'd like to take more," she said as though she were offering her life to him, and his stomach knotted. He'd never considered living his life with anyone else until that moment, and the thought scared the hell out him. It scared him more than what he was about to tell her.

"Are you sure? I could just leave. I could be out of your life in a matter of moments. Sophia didn't know anything about me other than that my situation at home was abusive and I ran away. I met up with someone who knew Pablo, and he arranged an audition for me. Pablo took me in, trained me, and made me a musician. He took care of me." He cringed at the mention of Pablo's name. The look in her eyes said she hadn't missed it. "Had she known, she never would have asked me to come here."

"She's not that shallow."

That was true enough. So, he began. "I grew up just outside of Chicago. We moved there when I was about eight, and Sarah was four. Dad had been fired from his job, and Mom thought we needed a change. At least that was what they told us."

Carissa took his hand and interlaced their fingers. Her eyes urged him to continue.

"I know now he was fired because he sexually harassed a woman at work. Her story didn't seem to hold up. She'd told everyone he sexually assaulted her, but it came down to harassment and they didn't send him to jail. They just fired him. Mom was embarrassed, and we moved."

He fidgeted in his seat. Carissa gave his hand a squeeze. "Things were quiet for a few years. He held a job, and Mom taught school. She taught at the same school we went to. I know now that was so she could keep track of us— and us of her. When I was eleven, he'd begun to accuse her of having an affair."

"Did she?"

He shook his head. "No, but I sure as hell wouldn't have blamed her." He ran his fingers through his hair and licked his lips. "He was a drunk. A mean one. You'd hear him lay into her with his words, then his fists, and then his body." He swallowed. "Why she didn't run away, I don't know except that I think she thought he'd kill her."

His heart continued to race. The story wasn't getting any easier to tell.

"It was that way for a long time. He'd beat my mom. Sometimes he'd beat me. It was bad enough a few times to stay home from school," he admitted. "Then there was Sarah."

He tossed the blanket aside and walked over to the piano that had once belonged to Millie. He pulled out the bench and sat down. He pushed back the wooden door that covered the keys, and his fingers ached when he did it. Gently laying his fingers on the keys, he played a few soft chords.

"Sarah was very small for her age. The night she died she'd turned twelve and a half," he recalled with a sad smile. "I'd written her a silly song, and she thought it was funny. Well, our father didn't like that." He turned on the bench and faced Carissa. "He'd never hurt Sarah before. Why on this night…" He ran his hand over his brow. "But we were sitting at the piano. She was just on the side of me." He looked to his side and could almost see her. "I'd finished the song, and she was laughing. She had such a beautiful laugh. My mother was standing behind us, and she was laughing, too. It was a beautiful moment." He shook his head. "He lost his job that day. I'd never seen him so drunk.

"He walked in and slammed the piano cover down on my hands." He swallowed again and pulled back his hands. The pain shot through them when he spoke. "He broke almost every bone in them," he said with a quiver in his lips. "Next he threw me back and began…" Tears were welling in his eyes. The man had meant to kill him. "My mother stepped in, and he threw her across the room. Then Sarah grabbed a vase. I think she meant to break it on him, like in the movies. But it didn't break until it hit the floor beside me. It just made him angrier."

He stood and crossed back to Carissa, who wept silently on the couch. Her mouth was wide open, and her eyes streamed with tears. He sat down next to her and wrapped the blanket back around them.

Immediately she took his hands and looked them over. She kissed each finger then shifted her gaze to him. He knew she still loved him. He'd been wrong to think the truth might push her away. She urged him to continue.

"He left me on the floor. I had glass on my face from the vase. My hands were wrecked, and he'd beaten me until my eyes were swollen shut. Sarah had run. My mother had run after her, and my father followed.

"I made it to my room and locked myself in the closet, just like I always did. I could hear him scream at my mother. I could hear Sarah scream. He was beating her, and my mother was trying to fight him." He closed his eyes tight. He could still hear her scream. "Then it was quiet."

Carissa wiped away her tears. "I'm so sorry," was all she could say.

He nodded. "I heard the sirens. Someone must have heard all the commotion." He kissed her hands that were still interlaced with his. "I woke up in the hospital. My mother said it took them two hours to find me. She could have lost us both."

"Sarah?"

"Died in her room at twelve and a half. He'd choked her to stop her from screaming. When she died, he ran off. They found him before they found me in the closet. They locked him up. I ran away."

"You ran away?"

He nodded. "My hands were still bandaged and my face was battered, but I left the hospital and I ran. I haven't seen my mother since then."

"Thomas…"

He shook his head. "It's okay." He mustered a smile. "I met a man who was a musician and was on his way to Paris. I followed. Three months later, I was auditioning for Pablo DiAngelo, and he saw to it that I finished my education and had a steady job."

"I think I need a drink." Carissa stirred to move from the couch.

"No. You don't need a drink." He pulled her back into his arms and held her close. "We can just hold each other."

She turned her face to his. "You don't drink." It was as though she finally realized it.

"I stopped drinking," he said. "Let's leave it at that."

"Thank you."

"For what?"

"For trusting me with this." She touched his face and skimmed her fingers over his jaw.

"I may have trusted you with it, but I can't change it. I will always be the son of a murdering, drunk bastard."

"So?" She shrugged.

"So?" His eyebrows shot up, and he stood. "So?" He paced. "Carissa, don't you understand? I can't fall in love with someone, marry someone, with his blood running through me. God, what if I hurt her—you? What if we had children and I..."

"Stop!" She stood up. "You're going to hide behind your father for the rest of your life?"

"I'm not hiding. I'm just staying away from situations that would allow me to become him."

"And you think falling in love, getting married, and having children would do that?"

"Yes." A storm brewed inside of him, and he wanted to shake her. Had she not heard a word he'd said? He wasn't the kind of man who could nurture and love. It wasn't possible.

"God, what have I done?" She moved through the room and toward the stairs.

"Where are you going?"

"To bed, Thomas. Alone," she added as she began her climb.

He grabbed hold of her hand. "I've scared you away, haven't I?"

"Excuse me?" She turned and looked down at him.

"Everything I've told you. It did just what I thought it would do."

"And what's that?"

"You're turning your back on me."

"No, Thomas, you did that to me. You've just told me that you will never fall in love, marry, or have children because your father was a drunk who beat you and killed your sister. Isn't that just what you've said?" His eyes were wide. "That's what I thought. So I'm okay to sleep with while you're under my roof, but I'm not someone you'd want to try to fall in love with. God forbid you should think about marrying me and having children." She swung her hair back over her shoulders. "Well, Thomas Samuel, that's something I want. I want to marry you and have your children because, dammit, I've already fallen in love with you. But that doesn't matter to you, does it?" She turned and ran up the stairs.

Thomas followed her, calling her name. Finally, she stopped at her door and turned around in such a fury that her hair whipped from one side to the other. He moved in closer to her. "You'll never know what it's like to be the child of someone who hates you. You don't understand that there is the possibility you'll be that person someday."

Carissa walked up to him and slapped him across the face. It stung. "If you'd stop feeling sorry for your damn self, you'd know that you are not the only person in the world with a fucked-up parent!" She held up her wrist. "Sometimes you have to hide the scars, Thomas. And other times, you have to show them to the world and say, 'Screw you!'" She turned back around and slammed the door.

He heard it lock, and his breath hitched. He'd bared his soul. It had hurt more than he had imagined it would. And Carissa, who'd promised she wouldn't change her mind, had.

He stood in the dark, silent, for a long time. Thinking about her scars. What was Carissa Kendal hiding?

She was gone when he woke the next morning. That wasn't really a surprise. However, when he got downstairs, he found Katie and Sophia having a cup of coffee in the kitchen. He turned his mouth up into a smile that felt forced.

"He rises." Sophia smiled and crossed the kitchen to pour him a cup of coffee. She handed it to him. "You look like you could use this. You always were a late sleeper."

"Yes, but that doesn't seem to bode well in this house."

"No, Carissa has been gone for hours. Left for a run. She looked a bit frazzled," Sophia added, and he didn't miss the motherly concern in her voice.

"I'll bet she did." He took a long sip of the hot coffee and let it warm his throat, which was sore from all the talking he'd done the night before and, no doubt, the screaming he'd done in his sleep.

He sat down next to Katie then stretched to give her a kiss on the cheek. "What are you two doing here?"

She was sitting in a wheelchair and he knew that couldn't have made her happy, but he'd never have known it from the look on her face. "I missed my house, dammit. I've lived here since I was born, and I missed it."

There was a tear in her eye, and Thomas placed his hand over hers. "Carissa misses you something awful, too. I'm sure if you wanted to come home…"

"I'm not coming home, but I damn well am going to come visit." She gave a regretful nod. "I'm old, Thomas. I fell, and I fell hard. I'm not dumb enough to think I should still be here."

"Carissa and I are here for you."

"Thank you." She patted his hand and held it there, over hers. "You two have each other, and something tells me you have a lot to figure out with that one. You certainly don't need me in the way."

Thomas nodded. He'd really screwed up, telling her about his family. He wished he hadn't, but what was he to do when he'd screamed in the night and shaken like a scared child? There was so much more he hadn't told her. How he had changed. What he'd become. Why he couldn't give into his feelings for Carissa. He'd realized this morning that he had to make her understand he wasn't a man she could love. She could trust him to be her friend and to help her with the dream of running her school. However, no matter how she felt, or how he felt about her, he couldn't let her love him the way she wanted to. It just wasn't going to be fair to her.

Sophia's stare caught him.

"She's at the school helping David with the drywall. They passed the electrical inspection."

"It's going so quickly."

"David had some time off. He decided to take it and get done what he could before he had to leave again. He seems to think if she can get her doors open before Christmas then some students could start during their winter break."

"That would be a good idea." Thomas finished his coffee and set his cup in the sink. "Maybe I'll go down there and see if they need some help."

"Grandma," Sophia stood, "I'm going to walk Thomas out. I'll be right back."

Katie nodded. "If Carissa gets some time in the next couple days, have her come see me."

"I'm sure she'll make it over this evening, and if not, tomorrow morning. You haven't been gone too long, but she sure misses you."

"I miss her, too."

Not having Katie at dinner on Sunday night had been obviously painful to each of them, even though they'd gone on and made the best of it. But Thomas had lived his life mourning a family and certain members of it. He knew

Katie, though she was just across town, was missed, and it was going to take a while to get used to the idea that she wasn't in the house, her television shows were not heard from the living room, and her cups of medicine weren't in the cupboard.

Sophia walked out to the car as she said she would, without a word, but Thomas knew her well enough to know what she was thinking.

"I broke her heart," he offered, and she nodded. "Sophia, there is so much I just can't give."

"I thought in all those years away from home you would have learned that loneliness isn't a way of life."

He snorted a laugh. "I agree."

"When did you stop drinking?" He turned his head with a snap. Her expression was neutral. "I've noticed, Thomas."

He swallowed hard. "Let's say it got a bit out of control. I had to fix it."

"Then you should be able to fix the rest. She fell in love with you the moment she saw you."

"She told you that?"

"I may not have given birth to her, but I am her mother. And she has secrets, too. Maybe you should compare stories, and you'll find they aren't too different." She walked away and left him wondering what Carissa's story was and why Sophia would want a man like him to love her daughter.

Chapter Nine

Carissa caught Thomas's eye before he even had the car in park. She was on a ladder, her father only feet away on another. Her hair was pulled up high atop her head in a ponytail, and a tool belt dangled from her hips. Damn, she was sexy.

His heart was already racing as he climbed from the car and neared the front door of the school. It was wide open. The October chill hadn't slowed the Kendals down. The entire school was almost drywalled.

"Thank God!" David hollered when he saw Thomas walk in. "I was just telling Carissa that if we had one more set of hands we could have this damn thing done by dinner." He was smiling, but his daughter was still looking at the wall.

David finished drilling the screws into his side of the board. He walked his hands across the wallboard to keep it in place before handing Carissa the drill. She drilled in to finish the area they were working on. She slowly started down the ladder, and David looked over at Thomas.

"I think she's a natural at this. Maybe you should go into remodeling work instead." Carissa gave him a shake of her head, and David laughed. "Well, I'm going to run down the street and get a couple waters. Need anything else?" he asked, but she shook her head again silently.

"Okay then." David left for the store, braving the cold without a jacket. Thomas was sure the tension between them was enough to drive anyone out into the cold.

Carissa dusted her hands against her pants and wiped the dust from her forehead. She looked up at Thomas, who was watching her, studying her.

"What?"

Thomas shook his head and gave a forced smile. "Your mom said you passed your electrical inspection."

"Uh-huh."

"What time do you start students?"

"Four."

"What time are you done?"

"Eight."

"Want to go to dinner after?"

"Thomas, why are you even bothering?" She rolled her eyes and dropped her shoulders.

"Carissa, this isn't how I want things. I didn't mean to hurt you by the things I told you about my life."

She held up her hand. "That's not what bothered me." Walking toward the back of the school, she pulled the belt off her hips and set it on a folding chair.

"Carissa, I never meant to upset you. It's too much to take in. I understand that. It's not like I want you to worry about my past. You have a school to build and…"

Carissa watched his eyes shift as he looked around the room.

He'd noticed the covered piano in the corner. "You got the piano?"

"Yeah, Mom talked the school into donating it. Imagine that." She wiped the back of her hand over her brow then looked up at him. "Go ahead."

"Really?" His lips broke into a thin smile.

"Yeah."

Before she could even help him, he had the cover off, the stool down, and he'd started to play. She could see him wince once in a while when a note wasn't just right, but she knew he'd fix that. He'd have the thing tuned in no time.

That would be good, she decided. It would give him something else to think about.

He'd perfected his art, and she now understood why. He'd channeled his life into his music. Every beating he ever took, every harsh word ever spoken to him, the life that his father took away from in front of him, filtered through his fingertips and into the music that flowed from the instrument. She was envious. She could make music, even make other's feel the song, but she couldn't put herself into a piece or even randomly string notes together to play the melody that was in her heart.

David walked back through the school and handed her a bottle of water. She thanked him with her eyes as they both sat and listened to the musician play.

Whatever was in his head were the notes that he played, not something he'd written or any piece she'd ever heard. It was what was in him. She almost felt a pang of guilt trickle through her. She'd stolen him to teach music, and he should be giving the world his talent.

A bit of envy flowed with the guilt. She'd never be good enough to play as he did. Her mother was, but not her. It had never mattered. She liked what she did, but she did envy raw talent like the one Thomas Samuel had.

It hit her at that moment that she would give anything to play with someone like Pablo DiAngelo just once. Just once to know what kind of power surged through a person to be with others so talented.

Then the guilt and envy settled, and determination washed through her. There had to be a way to make him learn to love. He deserved to love, and dammit, he deserved to love her.

When he stopped, it took her and David a minute to stop staring at him, mesmerized.

"I got a bit carried away," he said, pushing his fingers through his hair. "I tend to do that."

David stood and handed him a bottle of water. "Sophia used to do that, too. So does this one," he said, putting his hand on Carissa's shoulder and giving her a squeeze.

Thomas nodded. "Well, I didn't come here to play. I came to work. What do we need to do?"

"How do you feel about taping seams?"

Thomas's brows knit in confusion, and David put his arm around his shoulders and herded him toward the truck.

Thomas heard the whir of the drill as Carissa and David anchored more wallboards to the beams. David had given Thomas the specific job of taping the seams of the walls they had finished, but he struggled to grasp the concept of his new skill.

There wasn't a lot of chatter between them. At two thirty, Carissa said she'd better get home and get ready for her students.

"I'll bring Thomas home in a little while," David said. "If we can just finish that last wall, we'll be ahead of the game."

"Okay, that will be fine. Can I have the keys to my car?" She held out her hand, and Thomas produced them from his pocket. "Thank you." Their fingers touched, and finally, she looked him in the eye. Her cheeks were tear streaked, and her eyes were misty.

His heart slammed into his chest. Had she been crying all day?

"Dinner when you're done?" He lingered his fingers a moment more.

"I'm pretty tired."

"I'll have dinner ready for you then, when you're done."

She nodded, kissed David on the cheek, and left the two men in awkward silence.

David gave him the courtesy to have fifteen minutes of manly grunts and the scraping sound of drywall knives against the boards as they mudded the seams before he asked, "So what did the two of you fight about?"

Thomas was glad his feet were on solid ground and his work up on the ladder was finished. He wouldn't have wanted to fall from the highest rung of a ladder to his ass when David confronted him. "Just seems like we see things differently, that's all."

"Yeah, her mother and I did that for a while, too."

Thomas nodded and continued following David's lead, spreading drywall compound.

"What did you do? I mean while she was gone for so long?" He was curious how a man waited ten years for the woman he loved.

"I didn't think about it, really. Autopilot, excuse the pun." He smiled and Thomas, who still seemed to be in his own world, only nodded. "I had Carissa to raise, and when she came to live with me, she was a handful. I sometimes wonder if Sophia had stayed, if that would have driven her away anyway."

"Carissa was that bad?" He couldn't imagine.

"Not in her heart." David found his bottle of water and finished it off. He threw it into the trash can and settled his hand on the tool belt, adjusting it on his hips. "She's always been a good kid, but she tested her boundaries. She wanted to make sure finding me wasn't a mistake. She was seven years old and had been tossed around by her mother. Finally she found me, and she needed to know if I was just going to toss her out, too. As far as she knew, I'd already kicked her to the curb."

Thomas was bound to figure out what was wrong with Carissa if he could just ask the right questions. But he'd best tread lightly. "Why didn't you see her before she was seven? If her mother was so bad, why didn't you have custody of her?"

David laughed. "Sure as hell would have, had I known she existed."

And there was her issue with trust.

David continued, "Her mother told me she was pregnant with her when she was five months along. Right about the time she told me she was seventeen." He blew out a breath and shook his head in disgust. "Talk about thinking with your dick."

Thomas sucked in a fast breath, but David just laughed. "I was never that stupid again, I can guarantee you." He leaned against one of the walls. "She thought I'd marry her on the spot, but that wasn't what I wanted. If I was going to be someone's father, fine. I'd take that responsibility. I played and now I pay, ya know?" he asked as though he were testing Thomas.

Thomas nodded and hoped it was enough for David.

"Well, then she told me she lost the baby. She told me she had many medical bills, and I was more than willing to help with that. After all, I was the one who did it to her, as she kept reminding me." He took off the belt and hung it over a rung of the ladder. "After a few years, I got wise. Figured she'd had enough medical bills, and I went on my way. My aunt knew this girl." His eyes lit up, and he smiled. "The first time I saw Sophia, I fell in love."

Then he laughed. "Well, it was the second time, but my heart flipped in my chest."

David pulled a handkerchief from his pocket and ran it over his face. "I met her at Jeremy's wedding. She was cute, but young. Four years later, I was a pilot, and she was the most amazing musician I'd ever heard. She'd just auditioned for the symphony. I proposed to her three weeks after we met. She said no for three years."

"Three years?"

"She couldn't have her own children. She didn't want me to give that up. She felt like it was selfish to burden me with that."

"You didn't feel that way?"

"Hell no. Sure, I'd like to have had my own child. Who doesn't? But it didn't matter. There were thousands of children looking for homes. We could give a couple of them a family."

"She didn't want Carissa when you found out about her?"

"I'm sure you know Sophia well enough to know she's a little on the stubborn side."

"Yeah," he let out and then wanted to retract it, but David had nodded in agreement

"She left. She thought I'd lied to her about having a child. Truth is, she never stayed around long enough to ask about her. She didn't know I'd had no idea Carissa existed. So, for ten years I raised my daughter and pined for Sophia."

"What about her mother?"

"I took her in with Carissa. She needed more help than Carissa did, and Sophia had fled. I didn't take her back in a romantic way, but I took her in. When Carissa was ten, Mandy finally left. She'd wanted me to marry her, and I refused. She wanted me to get her a place of her own. I refused. Then she tried to commit suicide by slitting her wrists. Made a damn mess."

"And then she left?"

"More or less. She told Carissa that she'd hated her since she'd been born, and she was glad she had me to be a pain in the ass for. Then she left."

"No," Thomas breathed. And there was another piece. She had been told by a parent that she wasn't wanted. A parent who had done nothing but hurt her.

Heat rose in his cheeks. It was hard for her to trust because she hadn't had that early in life. It was hard for her to think anyone would ever stick around because those she'd loved, or those who should have loved her, had left. First her father and then her own mother had walked out. And the scar! Oh, the bicycle accident had scarred her, but he thought back to her expression when he'd first seen it. No one believed her. He knew it.

"Carissa's scar…"

"She wrecked on her bike, but anyone who knew she had spent the few years with her mother thought she'd tried to commit suicide. A counselor at school nearly decided to have her locked up."

"But she crashed?"

"Yep. Hid those scars until Sophia came around. I think they said they were warriors, and they uncovered them."

"The school"—he was digging for information now—"this is what she wants? This is what she's always wanted?"

David shrugged. "She's talked about this since she finished college. She's a certified music teacher." There was pride in his smile. "But she wanted to take care of Aunt Millie and Katie. I think she felt she owed it to them to be with them."

"Millie died shortly after you were married?"

"Her cancer came back. She was with us for two more years. It hurt Carissa for a long time. Then she began hovering over Katie, who doesn't like it as much as Millie did."

"She's afraid she'll leave her, too," he whispered as if it was an epiphany. "Didn't she ever want to play professionally?"

"Maybe once, but I think she was afraid to leave. Afraid...well, I don't know what she was afraid of. I would always have been here when she got back."

"Are we almost done?" Thomas unbuckled his tool belt and looked around the school. No longer was it an open space. It was taking form into small rooms just as Carissa had envisioned.

He could identify the walls he'd taped and mudded. They weren't as neatly done as those David had done. But he hadn't stopped him, so he must have thought he could work around his unhandy work.

"Sure. Let me get my things."

Thomas nodded anxiously.

David threw his things into the car and started the engine. "She sure fell for you hard and fast."

"What?"

"My daughter isn't an easy sell. But in just over a week, you've won her heart. She's so in love with you it makes me giddy."

Thomas let out a deep, long breath. How could two people have come from such messed-up lives and still think they could be good for each other? Neither one of them trusted anyone fully. How were they going to make it work between them if they couldn't trust each other?

There just seemed something so right about them. He and Carissa really did need each other. But he'd seen the look in her eyes. He'd belittled her experiences by dwelling on his own. It was selfish, but he'd fought it his entire life. How could he possibly think he could love someone? And now he wondered how she could possibly love him back.

As he'd promised, dinner was on the table for her when her last student left. She smiled as she walked through the door to the kitchen. She was sure she could get used to having him cook for her every day.

He pulled out her chair, and she sat down.

"Candles?" Her eyes shifted up to his and let a seductive grin cross her lips. "Are we going to be eating like this every night?"

"If I remember clearly, the last time we tried for a candlelit dinner, we didn't eat at all." He kissed her atop her head, and she nodded.

"No, I guess we never did get around to it, did we?"

"I hope you like tilapia. It's got a nice, lemon pepper zing."

"It smells great." She waited for him to sit down and then picked up her fork. "I wasn't very nice to you today. I'm sorry."

"I dumped a lot on you last night. You needed time to process it, and so did I."

"I don't think any less of you. I want you to know that."

"I know," he said, reaching his hand out to cover hers. "I learned a few things today. I'm afraid of becoming my father, yet you're nothing like your mother."

"Oh, I don't know. We're both a little anal retentive when it comes to our music. We both hover over Katie and Hope too much and…"

"Not Sophia," he interrupted.

"Oh." She laid her fork down and gathered her napkin in her lap. "My dad was talking, huh?"

"He didn't tell me anything he wouldn't have thought you would. I'm not sure he likes me that much."

"He likes you just fine." She lifted her hands out of her lap and took a bite of her dinner. "This is fabulous."

"Thank you."

"Another skill you learned in Italy?" She filled her mouth again, hoping to keep from talking about Mandy.

"Grandmother, actually. I was still pretty young when she died, but she taught me a few things."

"I'm glad she did."

She kept the conversation moving around in circles, avoiding anything that would lead to a conversation about her birth mother.

After dinner, they made hot chocolate and walked out to the covered porch. They wrapped themselves in a blanket and held each other close. It was romantic and peaceful, Carissa thought, until he began to ask questions.

"Tell me about your mother." She tensed in his arms. He was calling Mandy her mother, and she didn't consider her that.

"You know my mother."

"That's not what I meant."

"Why? Sophia is the only mother I'll claim." Her tone was defensive.

"Listen." He turned her so they would face each other. "You landed some heavy words on me. I wasn't looking for love when I came here. I have never in my life considered getting married or having a family." Her jaw clenched when he spoke. "Until I met you."

"You're just saying that because I was stupid enough to tell you I loved you."

"I'm telling you that because it's the truth. We said we'd each give a little. Now I'm asking you for a little. I want to know about your mother."

She gave a little grunt and sipped on her hot chocolate. "What do you already know?"

He told her what Sophia had told him. Then what David had told him. Carissa decided they hadn't left out too much except… "Both of them neglected to tell you she was a coke addict?"

She heard him let out a breath. "Yes, I guess they did."

"She used my dad, lied to him and to me. She bounced me around for seven years, telling me he'd left us." She snorted out a laugh. "Then when I find him, she moves her happy ass in." She shook her head. "That stupid stunt she tried by slitting her wrists just messed up my life, not hers."

He stroked his fingers through her hair. "You said once that the only good thing she did for you and your father was give you hope. What did that mean?"

She realized he hadn't understood the statement at all. "As in Hope Kendal, my sister."

"She gave you Hope?"

"Yes." She twisted so that her head lay against his chest.

"That's why you look alike. In the face, that is. Otherwise, you're strikingly different. You're dark and exotic, and she's fair and soft."

"Exotic?"

"Oh God, that hair, those eyes, the lips…" He laid a kiss on her neck. "Have you never looked in a mirror?"

"Thank you." She let out an easy, light sigh. She sipped her cocoa and led into her story. "She came back when I was seventeen. The same year Sophia returned to us. In two weeks, I fell in love with Sophia and wanted her for my mother. She and my father mended ten years apart and fell in love again. And then Mandy showed up." She felt him shift. "Mandy, my birth mother."

"Right."

"She was knocked up by some married man she'd had an affair with. She'd changed her name to Kendal and used the smooth line that she wanted her daughters to be together because she was dying. It worked on me like a charm, and it worked on Dad, too. He figured it was what he had to do. He told me once he was afraid that if he didn't, I would take off with the baby."

"Would you have?"

"I don't know. I never had to make that decision. He decided she deserved a home. He decided that at the risk of losing Sophia again."

"She didn't want the baby?"

"Please…" she laughed. "She'd left with Pablo, and we figured she'd never come back. But if she did, Dad would already have Hope by then. What kind of woman is met with the story, 'Hey my ex-lover had a kid. I'm going to raise it. Wanna be the mother?' and decides to stay?"

"Sophia, obviously."

"Well, she showed up just as Mandy went into labor. The look on her face when she heard him tell the paramedic that the baby was his…" She couldn't even explain. She took the Saint Nicholas medal that lay on her chest always and pulled it back and forth on its chain.

"Your birth mother…"

"Died in labor. She never saw Hope. Everything went as planned. She had Dad's name. He was named in her will as the person to get Hope. He was there, and his name is on her birth certificate. She is his daughter."

"And she's Sophia's daughter."

"Completely." She smiled. "She adopted us both on the same day. I was three weeks shy of eighteen when she legally became my mother. It was one my proudest moments."

"How long were they married before she legally became your mother?" His breath was soft in her ear.

"Three months."

"She's happy."

"I don't know if she has ever have been happier." She continued sliding the medal back and forth on the chain across her neck.

"What is this?" He lifted the necklace with his fingers.

"It was my engagement gift."

"Engagement?"

"Sophia asked me to be her daughter before she and Dad agreed to get married. Her mother had given it to her."

"That's precious."

"I would like to think I'd give it to my child, but I plan to have at least four of them. So who would get it? I think I'll give it to Hope when she turns ten. He's the patron saint of children. He'll keep her safe."

Thomas cleared his throat and shifted in the chair. "You want four children?"

"I do."

Carissa was fully aware of the awkward silence that fell between them. Marriage and children weren't even a subject he could be a part of.

She couldn't take away the pain and anger he felt from his childhood. She couldn't replace old memories or make them go away. Suddenly she wondered if she could ever love him enough to make him feel worthy. If she tried, she might have to give up her own dreams. Was that worth the price of love?

They slept in one another's arms. Things were in the open, though still touchy. They knew things about each other.

The school was coming together. They applied texture to the walls and installed the windows and doors. They would paint next, and then carpet and tile would be installed.

Carissa took on ten more students. Thomas started a theory class right in the study. Sophia even found she had three homeschooled students that wanted to learn cello, violin, and viola all at the same time. They made it work. It seemed like everything was coming together.

Halloween afternoon, Carissa had freed all her students to come another day. Thomas's only student was Hope, and then, as promised, her sister would take her trick-or-treating.

"Hope, go up to my room and get your costume on," Carissa called from the kitchen after she heard Thomas finish his lesson with her. "We'll eat, and then we'll go."

"Okay." She bounded up the stairs, and Thomas walked into the kitchen.

The aroma surrounded him as he wrapped his arms around Carissa's waist and buried his face in her hair. "Fajitas? Can't say I've ever had that at home."

"Hmmm, one of my specialties." She pecked him on the cheek.

They'd become comfortable. She refused to bring up the fact, again, that she'd fallen completely in love with him and he'd never reciprocated the words, but the feelings were there. She thought perhaps once the school was up and running, he'd ease up a bit. But for now, she'd settle for comfortable.

After dinner, Princess Hope stood at the door, her orange, plastic pumpkin primed with the four pieces of candy she'd already taken from Carissa's bowl.

"Hurry!" she yelled up the stairs at her sister as Thomas walked around the corner. "She's taking forever."

"What is she doing?"

"Changing."

"Changing?"

"Yeah, into her costume."

"Oh." He hadn't realized she'd be dressing up. Suddenly fantasies of Super Girl or Wonder Woman filled his head. He'd seen many costumes at the store. There had been that little French maid outfit and the devil. He felt his cheeks warm with his thoughts.

"Go get her," Hope whined, and he laughed.

"Okay."

Thomas hurried up the stairs and tapped on her door and opened it slowly.

Any fantasy of Wonder Woman was gone when he looked at her.

"Gypsy?"

"Every year I'm a gypsy, and Hope is a princess."

"This is a sister thing, huh?" He moved behind her and moved the mass of black curls from her neck. Hidden under the curls were large, silver earrings. "I like your hair like this."

"Do you?"

He pressed himself closer to her, and she let her body lean against his, feeling his intentions, and she smiled. "Thomas, I have to go beg neighbors for candy now." She turned to him, the bangles on her arms clinking as she rose them behind his head. "Meet me at my parents' house in two hours. Be nice to the kids, too."

"You're going to make me give out all that candy, aren't you?"

"Yes, and don't leave any. I open the bag one hour before people start knocking on the door so I don't eat it all."

"Maybe I'll throw the bowl into the bag of the first kid and call it quits."

"That isn't going to get me home and into bed with you any faster." She turned from him and grabbed up a shawl.

Thomas snagged her around the waist with his arm and pulled her to him. "Just tell me you won't change out of this outfit. I'd really like to have my palm read."

"I can tell you already what it says." She smiled wide. "You're trouble."

"I won't be any trouble at all if you let me take that outfit off of you myself."

She lifted up on her toes, gave him a gentle kiss, and went on her way.

The next morning, Carissa zipped up her suitcase and carried it down the hall. Passing Thomas's room, she noticed him sitting on his bed, his hands clasped in his lap. It was no secret. The trip to Chicago was weighing heavy on his mind. She wondered if perhaps she should go alone to purchase the school's instruments.

She stopped at the door and looked in. "Are you all right?"

"I'll be fine." He blew out a breath. "You're all ready to go?"

"Yeah, I'll just get this in the car, and we can leave whenever you're ready." She inched into his room. "If you don't want to go…"

"No. You didn't run away when I told you my story. I won't dismiss your trip. I just haven't been back to Chicago since I was sixteen." He let out a little laugh. "In fact, the only time Pablo performed there while I was with him, I faked a sickness so serious that he took me to the hospital. By the time I got there, I was so worked up they kept me."

Carissa felt sick to her stomach that she could hurt him by just making him go with her. "I don't want to cause you pain."

"Carissa," he looked up into her eyes, "I need to go, but I have a favor to ask."

"Okay." She stepped fully into the room and took his hands. "What?"

"I've never been to Sarah's grave. Will you go with me?"

Her heart slammed in her chest. She knew just how big a step he was taking. They'd been living comfortably, and his request moved them beyond that comfort zone and into a trust zone that hadn't yet existed. "I'd be honored." She smiled and pulled him to his feet. "C'mon. I'm hankering for Chicago pizza for dinner. If we get out of here in the next hour, we can have it."

He nodded, gathered his things, and they headed to Chicago.

Lunchtime found them at a truck stop in Des Moines. Thomas pushed his Dottie's Special Pot Roast around the plate with his fork. Carissa all but licked the ketchup from her plate once the fries were gone and the hamburger she'd chosen were history.

"It looks like I'm going to get that pizza for dinner after all," she said with a rise of her eyebrows, but Thomas's eyes never shifted. "I'd also like to go to the American Girl store and get something special for Hope tomorrow."

He only nodded.

Her heart ached for him. She felt she was dragging him along a painful journey, but she had to remind herself that he'd asked to go. After all, she'd offered him an out.

"Thomas," she waited for his eyes to shift to hers, "really, we can find you a place to stay, and I can go on by myself."

"I have to do this. I have to face it, Carissa. I cowered, and I ran." He pushed his full plate out of his way and gathered her hands in his. "I don't know what happened to my father or my mother after Sarah died." He brushed his fingers through his hair and then settled them back onto

Carissa's hand. "She tried to call me once. My mother, that is. I was in Paris."

Thomas squeezed his eyes tight. "Pierre was in the hospital there when she called. Pablo told her I didn't want to talk to her ever."

"How long ago was that?"

"About eighteen months ago, I guess."

"Thomas, she was reaching out to you."

"I know. I didn't tell Pablo to end the call. He was…he was angry with me, and that was his way of letting me know."

"We should find her. You could—"

"No." He shook his head. "I let that part of my life go. I need to move on."

When his eyes lifted to hers, she saw something and wished she could have captured it. His eyes sparkled. They'd actually sparkled, as if to tell her he was going to move on with his life and include her in it. She could have sworn the sparkle said I love you.

Heat rose in her cheeks, and she kept the smile that surfaced. Inside her heart flipped, her stomach clenched, and her mind buzzed. He loved her. It wouldn't be long before he told her so.

Carissa walked out of the lobby of the motel with the door key in her hand. Thomas stood, propped against the car. He still looked to her like Jimmy Stewart. He was so talented, so beautiful, and always just a little out of place.

"Okay, we're set. I got us a room with two beds." She kept a straight face as she approached him and headed toward the trunk to retrieve her suitcase.

"Good. You kick in your sleep."

"That's not me, pal, that's you!" The words flew from her mouth as a joke, but the realism of them hit her. "I'm sorry."

"If you're going to protect me for the rest of my life against my own feelings, it's going to irritate me." He moved to her and touched her cheek.

There was a positive statement there. "I want to protect you for the rest of our lives," she added softly.

"I'm fine." He brushed her lips with his. "Now, what time is your appointment tomorrow?" He kept his mouth hovered over hers.

"Eleven," she said on a sigh.

"Good." He scooped her up into his arms, cradling her against him. "What room?" he asked as he began carrying her toward the motel.

She laughed. "Put me down," she protested, but then nuzzled her lips into his neck. "Room one forty seven."

"Put the key in," he instructed with urgency as he held her.

She aimed the card toward the door, her lips still wandering a path against his neck. She slid it into the reader and sighed when the light turned green. She reached for the knob and twisted as Thomas kicked the door open with his foot.

"Ha! King-size bed. I knew you'd never sleep in a separate bed." With an approving nod, he laid her gently on the bed and lowered himself to her.

"What about the suitcases?" She was breathless beneath him as he lingered kisses on her neck.

"I'll get them when I'm done."

"Done with what?"

"You." He began to unbutton her blouse and started a trail of kisses down her body.

Chapter Ten

Carissa felt the chill off the lake blow through the buildings of Chicago as they walked out of the restaurant. Her head still spun from Thomas's kisses and touches from that afternoon, and they'd followed their lovemaking with pizza. She couldn't think of a better day.

"Oh, I don't think I've ever been so full in my life." She rested her gloved hands on her stomach and grunted.

"You had four slices of pizza. Chicago-style pizza isn't exactly a small meal."

"I'm happy. I'm so very happy." She wrapped herself around his arm as they walked toward the car. "Is it pretty here in the summer?"

"Yeah, it is. The lake is particularly nice with all the boats and people."

"I'd like to see it."

"Maybe this summer we can come back and go out on it." He opened the passenger door for her.

"Go out on the lake? Really?"

"Yeah. I still have a friend or two in the area. Roberto owns three sailboats. He'd be happy to let me borrow one, I'm sure."

"You can sail?" Her eyes were open wide with the information. He was opening up.

"Yeah, I can sail." He smiled down at her as he shut the door and walked around the car, opened his door, and climbed in behind the wheel. "So, now what do you want to do?"

Carissa turned fully to him in the darkness of the car. "I want to go back to the motel and do what we did all afternoon."

Thomas rested his head against hers. His eyes closed, and she felt him breathe her in. "You're not tired of making love to me?"

"I don't see that ever happening."

He only nodded as he started the car. Well, he wasn't sure about all that. Sooner or later things were bound to go awry. He'd yet to see a relationship withstand the word love. Even Sophia and David had thrown in the towel at one point. Carissa deserved to be in love with someone who wasn't as pessimistic as he was. He wanted be with her. She was everything he'd ever wanted in a woman, but what he had to offer emotionally was nothing. If it were possible to have learned to give himself to someone, he thought he would have by now. Until she decided he wasn't worth the time to love, he'd keep her close. He enjoyed the feeling of being wanted and desired, even if it wasn't going to last. He enjoyed everything about Carissa.

Carissa woke as the sun edged in through the motel's dark curtains. She squinted against its glare and turned toward Thomas. He was up and out of bed already. She let out a sigh.

She ran her hand over the sheets. They were cold. She listened but didn't hear him moving about the room. The realization that she was completely alone in the hotel room had her sitting straight up in bed. He'd left her. Oh God, he'd left her alone in Chicago. She'd thought he was opening up and beginning to love her, but instead he'd run.

She jumped from the bed and fell over the pile of clothes they'd tossed on the floor in their mad rage to get into the bed the night before. She pulled the sheet from the bed and wrapped it around her. The beating of her heart pounded in her ears.

When the door opened behind her, she caught her breath as Thomas entered the room. Her heart raced at a frightening pace and her lips quivered.

Thomas's eyes opened wide when he looked at her. "Are you okay?" He dropped the bag he carried and set a cardboard tray of coffee on the small table before reaching for her.

"I thought you left. I thought you'd run from me. I thought..."

"I told you. No more running." His hand was holding the base of her neck, and he'd wrapped the other around her. "Honey, I'm here."

"But maybe you'd had another nightmare and run out of the room. Maybe, just maybe, you didn't want to be with me. Maybe you'd realized I'm more trouble than you thought. Anywhere is better than with me." She fell against his chest, and he ran his hand over her hair.

"I'm sorry I scared you. I would never just abandon you." He held her tighter. "I did leave a note," he offered, and she pulled her head back to look up at him.

"I'm sorry. I panicked. I didn't even look for a note."

"It's all right. I just walked across the parking lot to the doughnut shop and got us some sweets for breakfast and some coffee."

"Thank you." She watched him pick up the bag he'd dropped and set it on the table.

"Carissa, tell me, why would you think I would go?"

"Everyone I ever loved left me. You're next. You're going to figure it out, Thomas. You're going to decide that your life is better off without me in it."

"I can't think of anything further from the truth. My life is certainly not better without you. Trust me."

She swallowed the sob that had rushed to her throat. "I'm just going to get some clothes on."

"Do you have to? I rather enjoy dining with you naked." He raised his eyebrows playfully, and she mustered a smile.

"Later." She turned to the suitcase, pulled out an outfit, and locked herself in the bathroom. She lowered the toilet cover and sat down. The sob that had caught in her throat turned into tears stinging her eyes.

Love. It wasn't an emotion she'd ever felt for anyone before. She raised her hand to her chest. Her heart still pounded.

She let out a breath and slowly got dressed. They had to meet with the instrument company, and then he'd asked her to go with him to the cemetery. If the morning was starting out as emotional as it was, it was bound to get even worse.

They arrived at their meeting at exactly eleven. The man that waited inside for them had almost fallen over himself when he realized that Thomas was indeed *the* Thomas Samuel.

"I'm a great admirer of your work. I cannot tell you how pleased I am to meet you." He continued to shake his hand.

"I really appreciate that." Thomas gave a nod toward Carissa. "And if you're familiar with my work, I'm sure you know of Carissa's mother."

The man turned to her. "Kendal?"

"I toured with her mother for years with Pablo DiAngelo. Sophia Burkhalter? She married a Kendal."

"You are Sophia Burkhalter's daughter?" The man's eyes lit up.

Carissa smiled. "Yes."

He clasped his hands together.

Carissa watched Thomas work magic. She'd fully intended to carry the meeting on her own, but the man was infatuated with Thomas and she was no fool to see that Thomas knew how to work him. By the time they were done, they had all the instruments Carissa had hoped to purchase and a library of theory books that Thomas had insisted on—all for less than she'd budgeted to spend.

Trying to be all business, she kept her excitement bottled until they pulled away from the store. "I can't believe you were able to get him to drop the prices."

"All I did was ask." Thomas grinned as he steered onto the street.

"Well, thank goodness you did. You saved us..."

"Two thousand and fifty-three dollars," he said, and she laughed at his precise number.

"Yeah, that." She lifted her hand to his, which lingered on the gearshift column between them. "Thank you."

"My pleasure." Then his face hardened, and he turned his attention back to the road, turning into a parking lot of a small floral shop whose displays filled the window. "I'm going to stop and buy some flowers."

Carissa nodded. She climbed out of the car and took his hand. She could feel his fingers tremble against hers. She gave his hand a squeeze to let him know she supported him.

Thomas appreciated the silence of the drive to the cemetery. He didn't know what to say if Carissa began to ask questions. He slowed the car as they approached the front gate. He pulled up to the information building and left the vehicle. Carissa didn't follow, and he returned only a moment later, handing her a slip of paper.

"Avenue A, plot 218?"

"The location of her plot. I told you, I've never been here. In fact, I didn't know if she was here for sure. This is where my grandparents are buried, my mother's parents. So I just assumed." He slid on his sunglasses and tried to blink back the tears that were already forming in his eyes. His mouth had gone dry, and his palms were wet. Being back in Chicago was hard enough. This might prove impossible.

He maneuvered through the cemetery as if he were looking for a house in a small town. She pointed out the sign that marked Avenue A, and he started down the narrow, tree-lined road.

Thomas pulled the car to the side of the road, cut the engine, and sat quietly looking out over the sea of headstones. One of them was his sister's. The image of the last time he'd seen her flashed through his mind. The happy moments they'd had sitting at the piano laughing blurred with the memory of his father chasing his sister and the fear in her eyes.

There was a pain in his chest. His first thought was to retreat, but then that was what he'd done when he'd left the hospital and run from his family. He watched as Carissa's hand moved from her lap and reached for him. He took a deep breath and kissed her fingers. "Let's go."

"Are you sure?"

This time he only nodded as he opened the door and stepped out onto the cold gravel road.

Her grave marker was small. It seemed appropriate. She was small. A mere child when she'd died.

Thomas brushed a tear from his cheek. Why hadn't he been there before? He'd always been there for his sister. Not only had he run from his life, but he'd run from her. He laid the flowers he'd brought for her just above her name. His stomach clutched. Carissa gave his hand a squeeze, and it reminded him he wasn't alone.

"Thomas?" A woman's soft voice carried on the cold breeze that blew through cemetery.

He stiffened, pursed his lips, and looked forward. Beside him, Carissa turned to look at the woman who had called to him. Two sets of footsteps approached behind him.

Carissa looked back at Thomas as the woman called out to him again. Finally, he turned. A woman walked toward him, a young girl at her side, their hands held together. The woman began to sob.

"Oh, Thomas." She released the young girl's hand and started toward him again, but stopped just short of wrapping her arms around him. "Thomas…"

"Mom," he said, but his voice broke.

Carissa's gaze wandered between mother and son. She could see the resemblance, and the trepidation, between them. It was painful. Again, she squeezed Thomas's hand, and he looked down at her. There was fear in his eyes.

"You've come to see your sister?" The woman who stood before them seemed to be searching for words. She had to be searching for a connection with the son she'd lost on the night she lost her daughter.

"I've never been here," he admitted.

"Oh, Thomas, I have missed you." Tears streamed down the woman's face, and Carissa could see her wanting to gather her son in her arms and hold him tight.

Carissa nudged him closer, but at that same moment, the girl who had been walking with his mother moved next to her and took her hand.

"I'm okay, honey. I'm okay." She patted the young girl's hand.

The girl, who Carissa supposed was about eleven, looked up at Thomas. She felt him shift his weight. She knew he'd seen the resemblance. The girl's eyes matched Thomas's and his mother's.

"Thomas, this is Madison." She shifted her eyes back to his. "She's your sister."

Chapter Eleven

Thomas felt the breath rush out of his lungs. He'd known she was his sister from the moment he had seen her. Eerily, she was the spitting image of Sarah.

"Dad…" was all he could mutter.

"I divorced him while he was in prison. He committed suicide the year after you left."

He needed to sit down, but there was no seat.

His mother wiped at her tears. "I couldn't be with a man who cost me both of my children. Oh, Thomas, why did you leave me? How could you have left me?" Her body shook with her words.

He watched. He ached. He wanted to run. Instead, he reached for his mother and gathered her in his arms. "I'm sorry. I'm so sorry." He held her against his chest.

Her tears soaked into his jacket. He breathed in her scent and whisked back to when she'd hold him and his tears would soak into her blouse. He remembered the night Sarah had died. His blood soaked into her blouse as well.

They stood in the cemetery. The air had cooled around them, but they held tight to one another.

When she could, Jane pushed back. Her eyes settled on the young woman visiting Sarah's grave with her son. A tightening in her chest made her force a smile. Was this his wife? Had he married without telling her? Did he have a family? Was she a grandmother? Oh, it wasn't fair that he'd left her out of his life.

Thomas reached for the woman's hand, and she walked toward them. "Mom, this is Carissa." Carissa held out her hand. "Carissa, this is my mother, Jane…"

He paused, his eyes seeking hers for confirmation.

"Jane Bennett," she provided.

Carissa shook her hand, but Jane could feel it twitch with nerves in hers.

"It's very nice to meet you, Ms. Bennett."

"Jane, please." She studied the woman who was obviously nervous in her presence. Thomas's eyes shifted between them as though he wanted her to accept the woman as someone he cherished. Trying hard to understand everything she was taking in, she smiled and asked, "Are you Thomas's wife?"

Carissa opened her mouth to speak, but no words came out. No, she wasn't his wife, but she was finding that she desperately wanted to be.

"Carissa is the daughter of one of the women I toured with in Europe," Thomas said, and Carissa felt the pain in her heart. She wouldn't expect him to say wife because she wasn't. However, he hadn't said girlfriend either. Hell, lover would have at least given the woman an idea that they had an intimate relationship. It was as though he'd dismissed her entirely, not even considering her a friend, and then he'd continued, "Carissa is a cellist. I'm helping her set up a music school."

As if the reunion of son and mother wasn't emotional enough, his words kept stabbing at her.

"You're a musician, too?" His mother looked at her, and Carissa nodded. It was all she could do.

Jane focused back on her son. "I called you a while back. Actually"—she sucked in a breath—"I called you every year on your birthday once I knew you were in Italy and Paris."

"You did?"

"Yes. I always spoke to…" She appeared to give it some thought. "Pablo?"

Thomas felt his lips press together. He'd thought Pablo had dismissed his mother because he'd been mad at him. But had he been protecting him for years? He shook off the thought.

"I called you after your accident. Oh, Thomas, I was so afraid I'd lose you before I could tell you how sorry I was for everything."

His head was spinning, and he saw Carissa take a step back. He hadn't mentioned the accident. He hadn't intended to.

"I followed you on the Internet so closely. When you were in that car accident with that man and they thought he'd die, well, I almost flew to your side. But when I called I was told that you didn't want me around." She wrung her hands, and Madison stepped up to her and took her hand. Jane clung to her daughter as though trying to take the strength and support she was offering. "I love you, Thomas."

Thomas took a deep breath. This was an opportunity to accept back what he'd run from. His father had died. Shaking his head he thought, what a coward. That blood ran through him. A coward's blood.

His jaw tightened.

His mother opened her purse and found a piece of paper. She took out a pen and wrote something out. "Here. This is my address. My husband and I live just outside Chicago. I added my phone number as well." She handed him the paper, and her hand shook. "Thomas, I'd like you to visit us. I'd like you to be part of my family again. You're my son," she reminded him. "I lost Sarah. I couldn't help that. She died in my arms." She sniffed back the tears. "I lost you. I could have helped that. I should have helped that." She reached for his hand. "I know what you think."

Thomas looked into his mother's eyes. They stared back. "You are not your father. Please, please never think that."

Thomas swallowed hard. It was hard not to think that, especially when he looked at his mother and then at his sister. Another set of eyes that matched Sarah's looked back up at him. He'd given up on family and the meaning of family years ago. He'd rejected the idea that he'd ever be part of one again, but he had been brought into one. Sophia and David opened their doors and their hearts to him. Carissa fell in love with him. He had a mother and a sister who wanted him to be part of their lives.

His heart raced again. It was like falling off of a bike and not wanting to get back on, but when you did you'd know what to do. He wasn't sure he wanted to ride again.

Carissa fumed in her seat as they drove back from the cemetery. When Thomas stopped the car, she flew out of the passenger side and into the hotel room. She pulled clothes from the rack and out of the dresser.

Thomas stepped through the door as she threw her belongings into the suitcase in a violent storm.

"Are you going somewhere?"

"Don't talk to me. Please don't talk to me."

"Carissa, apparently I've missed something." He closed the door behind him. "What are you so angry about?"

"Oh, Thomas, it's not worth even discussing. I want to go home. Our business here is done and we just need to go home."

Her voice cracked as she spoke. Her heart was breaking. She knew by the look in his eyes he knew he'd caused it, but he was too inconsiderate to understand why.

He grabbed her arm and pulled her toward him. "Stop."

She pulled against him, but it was no use. She didn't want to fight him, she wanted to love him, but he wasn't letting her. She collapsed against his chest and sobbed, trying to hold tight to what she wanted, but what he refused to give her.

He stroked his hand down her hair. "Now take a minute and tell me what the hell is wrong."

She took a few deep breaths and considered her feelings. Most of all she was upset with herself. She'd wanted him to introduce her to his mother as the woman he loved. However, the way he'd done it said she was nothing more to him than a daughter of an old friend. She'd felt betrayed. He held her when she slept. He consoled her when she was upset, yet he'd not been able to admit that he loved her or at least say he only wanted sex. It should be at least that simple.

And why had Jane Bennett wanted to fly to his side when he was in Paris? Who had almost died? What else wasn't he telling her?

When her breathing returned to normal, she looked up into his patient eyes. "Tell me you love me, Thomas. Tell me you want to be with me forever and that you want a future with me."

His eyes flew open wide and she began to sob again.

"Carissa, I don't think this is the time or place…"

"It never will be, will it?" She pushed her hair from her face and stepped back. She spun away from him and zipped up the suitcase she'd hastily packed. He stepped to her and touched her shoulder.

"Carissa, my feelings for you are so strong."

"Strong?" She turned back toward him. "Strong? That's not what I want, Thomas. What I want you can't give me."

"I told you that. I've always been honest about that."

She nodded. "Yes, you have. I can't believe I was stupid enough to believe it would change."

She picked up the suitcase and walked past him.

Carissa put her suitcase in the trunk of the car while he packed his suitcase. The thought had crossed her mind to drive away. To drive fast and escape anymore heartache, but she couldn't leave him. It hurt so badly because she loved him.

Thomas put his suitcase in the car and pulled the keys from her fingers. "I'll drive. You look like you could use the rest."

He walked to the other side of the car, and Carissa stood at the back. Perhaps it was better that she was angry with him. That way, when he gave up on her completely, it wouldn't matter. She didn't even want to drive back with him. That alone was going to be torture.

She walked around the car and pulled her door open.

"Why did you even come with me?" Her calm was gone as she slammed the door and turned toward him. "Why are you even still helping me with the school? What interest does it hold for you?"

He started the car and sat with the engine running. "I believe in the school, Carissa. I believe in you."

"You believe in me, but not enough to love me."

"I'm not the kind of man you want in your life."

"That's what you think. I heard your mother with my own ears. You're not your father."

"No, I'm worse." He tunneled his fingers through his hair and then gripped the steering wheel.

Carissa sat silently for a few moments. "Please tell me you respect me enough that you'll explain yourself."

"I will. And once we get back to Kansas City, I'm moving out."

She wasn't sure it was possible to feel your heart break, but she did. She felt it rip right in two. She'd wished he'd never come to Chicago with her, and that he'd quietly disappeared while she was gone. That would have been much easier to handle.

"Never mind. If you're walking out of my life, I guess I don't really need to know."

By the time Thomas pulled the car into the driveway, the sun was coming up. They hadn't stopped except to get gas. He'd bought them sandwiches at the gas station, but Carissa had refused to eat hers. When he put the car into park, she flew from the seat into the house and locked herself in her bedroom.

Thomas took his time gathering their belongings from the car. He walked her case to her door and set it just outside. He could hear her sobbing. His heart wanted him to knock on the door and apologize, but his head said run. Leave her to find what she needed, knowing he wasn't it.

He stepped away and walked down the hall to his room. His eyes burned from lack of sleep, and now they were tearing up. *Dammit, be a man. Men don't cry over women*, he told himself just as his father would have, but the tears broke free. The bottled-up emotions of going back to Chicago, seeing his sister's grave, and hearing his mother's voice crashed through him. He sat on the edge of the bed and cried.

It all hurt, but the worst was knowing he'd broken Carissa's heart.

The woman loved him, and dammit, he loved her. Why couldn't he just accept that?

Because he knew, in the end, her hurting now would be less than when he hurt her later. If he told her he loved her and they moved forward, things would just get worse. What if someday he touched her, hurt her, perhaps—oh, God—even killed her?

He lay back on the bed and closed his eyes. Then he reached his hand into his pocket and pulled out the slip of paper his mother had given him and his cell phone.

With trembling fingers, he dialed the number she'd written down.

"Hello?" A sleepy voice answered. Thomas looked over at the clock. It was only six in the morning. He'd wakened her.

"It's Thomas," he said softly.

"Thomas!" Her voice was fully awake now. "Oh, I didn't think you'd call."

"I'm sorry for waking you."

"No. No. You call me anytime." Her voice was shaky, and he knew she was crying. "Are you still in Chicago?"

"No. I just got back to Kansas City."

"Is that where you live?"

He let out a sigh. "For the moment." He scrubbed his free hand over his unshaven chin.

"Mom, I'd like to come visit for a few days."

His mother lived in a nice house. There was a Lexus and a BMW in the driveway of the two-story home with the porch light on. He climbed from the rental car and stood in the street, taking in the view.

The house they'd lived in when he was a small child had nearly fallen in around them. The house he'd fled from and never returned to had been a block from a run-down bar, with furtive strangers exchanging money for small packages on street corners.

Jane Bennett opened the front door and stepped outside. She seemed so much older than when he'd left so many years ago. He thought too, the man who walked toward her now certainly wasn't the young man whom she remembered as her little boy or whom she'd held, bleeding against her on the floor of the closet.

She ran her hands down her arms as though fighting off the chill. He saw the wedding ring on her hand as he neared. Whomever she'd married had been someone much different from his father. Clothing, jewelry, cars, and a beautiful house fitted her. As a young man, he'd always wished such wonderful things for his mother, wished he could give them to her.

"Thomas, I'm glad you've come." She smiled, and he felt his chest tighten. As he cleared the last step and stood face-to-face with her on the porch, she held out her arms and he fell into them as though he were still that little boy.

"Oh, Mom, I've missed you. I've missed so much." He sobbed against her shoulder. She raised her hand to his head and stroked his hair. He gasped a breath when he realized he was home.

"I've missed you, too," she said softly against his cheek, and suddenly all the nights he'd spent being so alone and scared disappeared. She missed him. She'd wanted him back, and now he was.

When he could finally breathe and the tears had almost dried, he took a step back. His mother held tight to his hands and looked him over. He'd been a skinny boy, shy, with no confidence. He hoped that she'd see he wasn't a weak child anymore, and that she'd look at him as a strong man, a man of the world. Strong, not in physical strength like his father, but in heart, like she was.

"Come inside." She took his hand and led him into the well-furnished home.

The young girl he'd seen at the cemetery sat on the couch watching television. She stood when she saw him walk through the door with their mother.

"You remember Madison?"

"I didn't get the chance to say hello." He held out his hand, and she shook it timidly.

He couldn't help but stare at her. Her eyes, her hair, her build all matched Sarah. His mother patted his shoulder, obviously knowing what was going through his mind.

A man emerged from the other room. He was tall, at least as tall as Thomas. His hair was white, and even lounging in his home, he wore slacks with his T-shirt tucked into them. A heavy, white mustache shadowed his top lip. Thomas figured he was at least ten years older than his mother.

"Thomas, this is my husband, Parker Bennett."

"It's a pleasure to finally meet you, Thomas," he said, holding his hand out for him to shake.

Acceptance, Thomas realized. It was something he'd never had from his own father. Reeling at the unexpected welcome, he shook the man's hand.

"Why don't the two of you go into the kitchen? I just made a pot of coffee, and Madison and I are going to head upstairs," he offered, pausing as Jane kissed his cheek. "Thomas, it was nice to meet you. I hope you'll be visiting for a while." He smiled and escorted his daughter up the stairs.

"I can't believe…"

"How much she looks like Sarah?" They watched them disappear to the second floor.

"Yes."

"I will admit there are days I find myself calling out the wrong name. I know she's used to that. But I feel bad about it." She looked up at him. "She's very familiar with both of you. I've made sure she knows about her brother and sister. I'd always hoped you'd return."

"I should have been back a long time ago."

"You're back now." She patted his arm as she walked him to the kitchen.

Thomas sat at the table while his mother poured them each a cup of coffee. He looked around the kitchen. He recognized a few of the small artifacts that sat on shelves or hung on the wall. They'd been part of his home, years and years ago.

Jane turned from the counter and let out a small, nervous laugh.

"I just realized I've never prepared a cup of coffee for you. How do you like it?"

"Just black is fine."

Jane carried the mugs to the table and set them down, then pulled out the chair next to Thomas. She could still see the boy that had been so frightened. The image of him hiding in the closet, bloodied and unconscious, had kept her up nights and had disturbed her dreams. Now a man sat in the shadow of that little boy. Her little boy.

"Where is your friend?"

"Carissa?" he asked, and she nodded. "Back in Kansas City. She's home."

"She seemed like a lovely girl. Just a friend?" She held on to her coffee mug as she eased into a conversation with her adult son.

"I'm sure you know she's very special to me." He rolled his mug between his hands. "She's told me she loves me."

Jane sucked in a breath of pride. This woman loved her son, and what wasn't there to love? "I could see that she meant a lot to you, and you to her."

"Well, we haven't known each other very long, and quite frankly..."

"You're too afraid you'll hurt her like your father hurt all of us."

He let out a sigh. "Yes."

Jane put down her mug and placed her hands over her son's. "The alcohol did that to him. He wasn't always that way."

"It's the only way I remember him."

She nodded, understanding that. "We were married four years before you were born. He was a hardworking man who had a thirst for success."

Jane saw his eyes change as he shook his head. She realized he didn't know that man. "I know, that's not the man you think of when I talk about him that way." Thomas nodded, and Jane felt the sadness of it down to her stomach. "We lived just off the lake in a beautiful apartment downtown," she reminisced, thinking of their first home together. How young, happy, and in love they were once. "He showered me with gifts, and he wrote poems." She smiled at the thought, and feeling heat in her cheeks, knew she'd blushed.

Thomas shifted his head, and the confused look that crossed his face had her laughing. "Yes, believe it or not, your talent comes from your father. I have no talent," she laughed. "He, at one time, was an amazing person."

Jane released her son's hands and eased back in her chair. "When I found out I was pregnant, he panicked. He began withdrawing our savings and investing heavily. I was young," she said with a shake of her head. "I didn't realize what he was doing. I thought he was just trying to do right by our pending family." Her eyes shifted to his. "He lost everything he'd worked so hard for. We had to move. I had to get a job, and he began to drink."

She sat up and drew in a deep breath. She hadn't thought about her first husband in years. Not in the way she was thinking of him now.

"I suppose I should have known that he had it in him to lose control. He obsessed about everything. The good and the bad. The house was never clean enough. The car never ran just right. Even the weather was never the right temperature." She shook her head. "He was never completely happy. Knowing others depended on him made things worse. He never had control over you or Sarah like he did over me. That was my own fault. I see that now."

Jane noticed her cup was empty. She stood and walked to the coffee carafe, then carried it to the table and filled her cup. When she held it out for Thomas, he shook his head, and she put it down on the table.

Thomas was a handsome man, she thought. He had outgrown the awkwardness that had only fueled her husband's disdain for him. She wanted to help him understand that many things had contributed to his father's abusive behavior.

"Things never got easier. He got more run-down, and our family suffered. He hit me for the first time when you were six. He hit you for the first time shortly after that." Guilt rose in her and threatened to strangle her, like it had for years. She should have stopped it then, she knew. Taken her son and run, but she'd stayed.

When he saw the tears form in his mother's eyes, he took her hand and gave it a squeeze. He'd come to find himself, to reconnect, to get answers. He'd hoped his travels hadn't hurt his mother more.

"I stopped drinking a little over a year ago," he admitted. He saw her raise her other hand to her mouth to keep in her sob. "Things had turned, and that's where I turned. Just like him."

He raked his fingers through his hair and then scrubbed them over his face. "I hurt myself, nearly killed my friend, and destroyed a relationship that meant the world to me. I killed my career. Now my past, my mistakes, hold me back from the woman I love."

"So you do love her?" When he nodded his response, Jane smiled. "Why should a past mistake hold you back?"

"I lost control, Mom. I nearly killed a friend and myself. What's to stop me from hurting her physically? Just by being here, I know I'm hurting her."

"But hearing you talk, I know you've learned from your mistakes." She reached for him, placing a warm, soft hand on each side of his face. "We've all made mistakes. We will all make more of them." She smiled through her tears. "Look around you." She dropped her hands. "I've moved on from mine. And trust me, when you lose a child so violently, it's hard to move on."

Jane stood and paced the kitchen. "Oh, Thomas, I lost so much that night." She covered her mouth and sobbed.

He stood and gathered his mother in his arms and held her.

She wrapped her arms around him and held him tight.

"I lost both of my children and my husband that night. Everything I'd known and loved was gone."

"I'm sorry, Mom. I'm so sorry."

"Please tell me you're back in my life." She looked up into his eyes. "I can't lose you again. It was too painful the first time."

He held her tighter to him. "I didn't mean to hurt you so much."

"I know, but you're back now." She kissed his cheeks.

"I should let you get on to bed. Your family needs you."

"You are my family," she reminded him. "Do you already have a place to stay?"

"I was going to check into a motel. I thought I'd stay a few days and catch up. I need to decide what I want to do, and I need time to let Carissa simmer. I owe it to her to, at least, go back and let her tell me she doesn't need me in her life." He let out a laugh. "My guess is that I'm fired."

"You're selling her short."

He didn't have anything to say to that. Maybe he was.

She took his hand and led him through the house. "C'mon, I have something to show you."

There was a small home office, a washroom, and a white, six-panel door that closed off another room.

Jane stopped in front of the door and looked up at him before she pushed it open.

His eyes flew open as he stepped over the threshold of the room. "Oh-my-God." He let out the breath he was holding. "These are all my things."

Jane nodded as she watched him. This room was a collection of his and Sarah's childhood. The material items that had once been important.

His rocking horse from when he was a toddler and his Matchbox cars were there. Sarah's teddy bear and her princess wand sat in a small rocking chair next to the bed. His bed.

How many hours had Jane sat in this room and mourned the children she had lost—the life she had lost?

Thomas looked at her again, and she smiled a warm, gentle smile. It had been worth it to her to save their things so that she'd have them near.

She picked up a doll that sat on the dresser and stroked its hair. "I brought everything that was yours and Sarah's with me. Parker made sure the house we bought would have an extra room for you when you came back." She looked up at him. "And here you are."

Carissa wandered through her day at the school, exhausted after having stared at the ceiling of her bedroom all night long. The carpet was down in the parents' area, and the laminate wood floor had been finished in the rest of the school.

She'd opened the door just in time for the shipment of instruments to arrive. Things would be ready for the school to open within a week. It was much further ahead of schedule than they had planned. The thought should have made her happy, but instead, the opening of the school and the enrolling of students had tears welling in her eyes.

Carissa fell into one of the parent chairs and stared at the boxes that cluttered the room. She rested her elbows on her knees and her face in her hands and looked around. There was no desire to tear into them and fondle every instrument. She simply wanted to crawl into the corner and sob.

"Excuse me," a man's voice called to her, and she snapped her head up. She hadn't even realized anyone had walked in, and there stood the stranger only feet from her.

She stood and looked him over. He wasn't tall, but dark and handsome fit the bill. Wavy, dark hair covered his head, and the shadow of a beard darkened his chin.

"I'm looking for Sophia Burkhalter." He shook his head. "Sorry, Kendal. I'm looking for Sophia Kendal."

The accent should have given him away, but it took Carissa a few more moments of carefully studying the man to realize who he was.

"You're Pablo DiAngelo." Her eyes widened as she let the name roll from her tongue.

"That's what they tell me," he said, and his smile winked a dimple in his cheek. "And now we are at a disadvantage. You know me, but I do not know you."

She held out her hand. "I'm Carissa Kendal."

"Ah, bella!" He bent in and kissed her on one cheek and then the other. "You are a beauty. An absolute beauty!"

A smile finally slid across Carissa's lips, and her tears dried. "Thank you. My mother should be here any moment."

"Mother. Not a word I associate with my dear Sophia, but I'm sure she wears it well."

"Yes, she does."

"So..." He scanned the school from where he stood. "What have we here?"

"This is my school." She swung her hand through the air. "It'll open in a few weeks. We just received our instrument shipment." She looked at the boxes that surrounded them. "It's my chance to pass music to others."

"Your mother and father are very proud, yes?"

"Yes." She swallowed back the disappointment that Thomas wasn't there to see his old friend and show him their pride and joy.

"Oh my! Pablo?" Sophia's voice came from the door, and a moment later, the gorgeous Italian turned and scooped her into his arms.

"Bella! Oh, my bella!" He set her on her feet and looked her over. "You are happy?"

"Oh, Pablo, I've never been happier." She looked across at Carissa. "You've met my beautiful daughter?"

"Si, she's a beauty." He took another long look at Carissa and then back to Sophia, who stepped to the side when Hope tugged at her blouse.

"Oh, Pablo, this is my other daughter, Hope."

Carissa's little blonde sister looked up at him, and his dimples creased his cheeks. "Hope, it's so nice to meet the young girl who took this talented woman away from me."

Hope drew her eyebrows together. "Away from you? I thought my daddy took her away from you."

"Hope," Sophia silenced her.

"Yes, he did. Your mother loved him more than she loved me," he said with a hint of humor in his voice.

"She loves my daddy very much."

"She always did." He shifted his eyes back to Sophia.

"Why are you here?" Sophia took his hand and led him to a chair.

"I'm here looking for you." He rested her hand on his knee and then covered it with his own. He took a deep breath. "We've been invited back to the Vatican."

"Oh, Pablo!" Sophia flew from her seat and wrapped her arms around his neck. "Oh, God! That is wonderful!"

"It's like the encore performance we never got. I've come back for you, bella. Tell me you can come with me. Your husband should be able to handle everything for a few weeks."

"Oh, Pablo, I can't." She sank back into the chair beside him. "I haven't played seriously for eight years. Oh, you don't want me."

"Of course I want you. You're all I have left." There was an anger brewing in his eyes. He stood and paced the small area, raking his fingers through his hair. "I need you."

"But Pierre? Thomas?" she asked, and his face hardened as his brows drew together.

"No! No! Pierre can't play, and Thomas…" He threw his hands in the air. "I want only you. If I can't have you, I walk."

"Pablo, wait." She stood and rested her hands on his arms. "I can't go, but I know someone who can."

She turned toward Carissa, who stood just a step away, her mouth gaping open.

"Me? Oh, no. He wouldn't want me."

"I wouldn't want her," he repeated. "I want you."

"And who do you think has taught her everything?" Sophia raised her brows. "Listen to her play."

"Mom."

"Carissa, go get your cello," she instructed without shifting her eyes from Pablo's.

Carissa hesitated for a moment then retreated to the back of the school and returned with her instrument.

"Now sit," Sophia told Pablo and turned to Carissa. "Il mio perso amore."

Carissa nodded and took a deep breath. She closed her eyes for a few seconds and then pulled her bow across the strings, letting out the first low note. Pablo straightened in his seat.

Carissa's body moved into the cello, and her mind filled with the music. Her eyes closed, and the world fell away. The notes flowed from the instrument as though she were making love with music.

When the last note faded, Carissa lowered her bow and shifted her eyes to her mother, who merely smiled.

Pablo sat quietly and kept his eyes steady on her. He made her nervous. There wasn't a sign on his face that said he loved or hated the piece she'd played. Then slowly his dimple appeared in his cheek, and his lips spread into an enormous smile.

"You will play the Vatican with me."

"Me?" Her voice shook with the absurdity of the conversation. "But my school. What about…"

"You come." Pablo stood. "Bella, you will take over the school until she returns. I want her with me."

Sophia smiled with a nod, batting away what Carissa knew were tears of pride, but she wondered if they were tears of pain as well.

Sophia had wanted to play the Vatican. She'd spent ten years playing with Pablo DiAngelo, trying to earn that coveted invitation. It had never come until Sophia had given her heart to David and Carissa. Pablo had come back for Sophia, and she'd gone. Had they played the venue, which had then been canceled, everything in Carissa's life might have been different.

Carissa felt the pang of guilt pierce her. She'd thanked God for taking away Sophia's chance to play at the Vatican because it had sent her home and they had become a family. And now, unselfishly, Sophia was giving the opportunity to her to live out. He'd offered the position to Sophia, and she'd refused it.

The pang of guilt pierced further into her before she noticed the look in Sophia's eyes. It was the look of love— love that she had for Carissa. Just as a mother would, she'd give up her dreams for her daughter and hand them to her to fulfill.

Carissa swallowed hard and fought the tears that stung her eyes. Not only was it a chance to do something new and exciting, a chance to leave Kansas City and the thoughts of Thomas and what might have been, it was a chance to fulfill Sophia's dream for her.

Still, she wasn't sure she could do it. She'd never left home before, or the people she loved. Hope needed her, and so did her parents. What about Katie? Katie was her responsibility. And what if Thomas came back?

She sucked in a breath. They'd all be there when she got back, wouldn't they?

They agreed he'd come to the house for dinner and they would discuss everything, but Carissa found that there wasn't much discussion with Pablo DiAngelo. Either you agreed with him, or you simply didn't speak to the man again.

Pablo filled the dinner discussion with plans he had to carry out the performance.

David reached his hand to Carissa's and gave it a squeeze as she processed what was being said. "Carissa, you do what you want," he interjected.

Carissa could feel her forehead tighten as she drew her brows together sharply. She knew what she wanted to do. She just wasn't sure she could.

David watched her closely. She knew he could read her thoughts. That's what fathers did. That's what her father did.

On a sigh, with a tilt of his head, he said, "But think about the opportunity. It is the one venue your mother always wanted, and it's being offered to you. The school will be here when you return. And it wouldn't look too bad for the credentials of the teacher to have played the Vatican."

Carissa sat silently for a moment and contemplated what they'd all said. She'd never played a big venue like Sophia had once been used to. Could she even compete with the talent that would build his ensemble?

Her heartbeat settled when she realized Pablo wasn't the kind of man to ask her to join him if he didn't think her talent was good enough.

The school wasn't open. She had no man in her life and her family supported the opportunity. She would be a fool to not take it.

Carissa lifted her head and sucked in a breath. "Pablo, exactly how long would I be in Italy?"

Pablo lifted his wine glass in a salute. "Ah! She comes to her senses. We leave in the morning and rehearse for two weeks. Then we give the concert."

"Why now?" Sophia asked. "Why did they relent after all these years and ask you back?"

A pained expression flickered in his eyes. "New pope."

Sophia walked Pablo to the limo that waited for him. Only Pablo DiAngelo would think he'd need a limousine in Kansas City when a rental car would have done, she thought. The sun had set, and the temperature had taken a dive. She held tight to his arm and rested her head against his shoulder as they walked.

"I've missed you," she said softly.

"Ah, bella, I've missed you, too. Pierre misses you as well." He turned to her as they reached the car and gathered her hands in his. "Are you sure you won't come, too?"

"I can't. I shouldn't have gone the last time you came for me. I'm needed here, Pablo. I hope you understand."

"Of course I do. Love is an amazing thing."

"It is." When he pulled her to him, she let herself fall against him. "Who will you use in your ensemble?"

"I have a couple others in Rome. It won't be the same," he said with a painful sigh. "But it will be good. To have Carissa will be amazing. To tell all that this is Sophia's daughter…well, that alone will be brilliant marketing." He laughed.

"Why not Pierre? You said he couldn't play?"

Pablo shook his head violently. "I don't speak of it. He was hurt. He's not in the best shape, bella."

"I didn't know." She gently touched Pablo's cheek.

"Well, then you live under a rock." His statement was angry, and Sophia knew better than to ask about it.

"What about Thomas? He was the best and—"

Pablo's hand came up between them, and even in the dark of the night, she saw his eyes grow black in fury. "That name is dead to me."

"Pablo…" Her eyes opened wide as she gasped his name.

"Goodnight, bella." The driver opened the door, and Pablo climbed into the car and shut the door without another word. The driver tipped his hat to Sophia, and they drove away.

Sophia stood on the sidewalk, watching the taillights of Pablo's car disappear. She needed more time with him. Something had transpired between those she loved, and she didn't know anything about it.

Carissa walked down the front steps and to her mother. "Are you okay?" She rested her hands on Sophia's shoulders.

"I'm fine." She turned and saw Carissa had her jacket on and her purse on her shoulder. "Are you leaving?"

"Yes. I guess I have a lot of packing to do before tomorrow." She smiled, but Sophia saw through it.

"Are you sure you want to go?"

"I have to go. I have to leave and see that I can survive the one thing I've always been afraid of." She wiped away the tears that rolled down her cheeks "I have to accept that Thomas is gone and he's not coming back, and that I can go on. That you'll all be here when I get back. I have to prove to myself that I can survive."

"Is this the way to do it?" Sophia laid a gentle hand on her daughter's shoulder. She felt her shake as she fought back emotions that Sophia knew she struggled with.

"I'm going. I have to do this. I told him I loved him, and he ran. He's not coming back. We made a mistake, Mom. Thomas Samuel wasn't the man for the job."

Sophia shook her head. She didn't believe that.

"Carissa, don't give up on him yet. You don't know what he's going through."

"What I know is he's not here to celebrate this moment with me." She tossed back her head, and her hair fell back behind her shoulders. "All I know is he's not in my house, his room is empty, and he couldn't even tell his mother I was more than just the daughter of an old friend."

Sophia cringed and pulled her hand back. "Oh, Carissa, I'm so sorry." She was so much more than that to Thomas, and Sophia knew it. It pained her that he'd have chosen his words so that Carissa would hurt so badly.

"No, no. I don't want to be sorry for myself anymore. I'll be back in a few weeks. I'll have lived a wonderful dream. How many people can say they played at the Vatican? I'll be able to say that. I will be able to hold my head high, come home, and teach those who want to learn how to make music. And I can do it without a man. I can do it without Thomas."

Carissa huffed out a breath. "I'm a warrior, right?"

Sophia nodded, remembering the bond they had made eight years ago when each of them had shared their physical scars with the other.

Carissa pulled at the Saint Nicholas medal that hung from her neck and held it in her hand. Sophia felt the twisting of her heart when she watched her daughter hold tight to the medal her own mother had given her to protect her. Carissa cherished it as she had.

Carissa squeezed her eyes tight then looked at Sophia. "This is just another scar to bear. Right?"

Sophia took her into her arms and held her.

She'd said she could do it without a man, but was that really what her daughter wanted? Sophia didn't think so. All signs led to Carissa being miserable without Thomas, and if she knew Thomas, he was miserable without Carissa.

As the matchmaker, she had learned, the pain felt by the pair was felt by the one who put them together.

Chapter Twelve

Thomas woke in his childhood bed for the third time, and yet he'd still not swallowed the fact he was in his mother's home. A nightmare had crept in the first night he slumbered under her roof. She'd heard him, and so had her husband. They had come to him, held him, and comforted him.

"I have them, too," his mother confided in him. "I've been through therapy. I've been on medications. I've had people sit by my side on suicide watch." Thomas's eyes flew open at the mention of suicide. "I had nothing, Thomas. I lost my husband. I lost my daughter. I lost my son."

Thomas dipped his head like a small child who was in trouble, but his mother lifted the face of the man with her finger and kissed his cheek. "But he's home now, and I'm going to take care of him."

"I don't know how to accept any of this."

"First things first. You know you are welcome in our home. We are your family. You have a sister who wants to know you." She took a breath. "Next you're going to go back to Kansas City and help that beautiful woman get her school open."

Thomas shook his head. "She isn't going to want me."

"Then," she continued, "you're going to learn how to forgive and how to ask for forgiveness yourself. You love her."

"I didn't tell her that."

"No, but you do. You love her very much."

He nodded. He did love Carissa. His heart wouldn't ache so badly if he hadn't fallen completely in love with her.

Now he'd walked away. He'd left just as he'd promised he wouldn't. How was he going to go back and expect her to understand when he had done to her just what she feared he would?

Thomas sat on the front porch and soaked in the sounds. Back in Kansas City, if he were sitting on the porch of the house Katie grew up in and Carissa now lived in, he'd hear music. Cellos, violins, piano, and even one little girl who tried her hardest to hold onto to her tuba would be making music. Chicago, however, was silent, void of all of those sounds he'd become accustomed to.

"I brought you some hot chocolate," a small voice in the doorway said.

Thomas turned to see Madison standing there in her pajamas, slippers, and heavy winter coat, holding two cups with marshmallows dancing on top. The smile that spread over his lips was genuine. "Thank you."

"It's really cold out here," she said, handing him one mug.

"It is. I didn't realize just how cold until you brought me this." He held the hot drink between his hands. It warmed him almost as much as the gesture from his sister had.

"Mom says she liked lots of marshmallows in her hot chocolate." Madison inched closer. "Sarah, that is. Mom said she really liked sweets."

He nodded. "She did. Her favorite was chocolate Easter bunnies."

"I love chocolate Easter bunnies, too." She moved to the chair next to him and sat down. "I have a picture of the two of you in my room. Would you like to see it sometime?"

"I would."

"Mom said it was taken on Halloween before she died."

His breath hitched. Thinking about Hope dressing up for Halloween and the beautiful gypsy that Carissa had transformed into, he swallowed the lump that had formed in his throat.

"She was Cinderella," he reminisced. "I was Prince Charming."

Madison nodded. "I'm always a superhero."

He laughed. "Which one?"

"Oh, last year I was Wonder Woman. My dad picked her because she was his favorite. Do you know which one she is?" Her eyes had opened wider, and her voice lightened.

"I do. My favorite was always the Incredible Hulk. He's really strong."

"Yeah, but he's green."

"But he's strong."

"Did you dress up for Halloween this year?"

He shook his head. "No, I was the candy passer-outer."

"At your house?"

Thomas finally took a sip of the hot chocolate she'd brought him. He was glad it was hot enough to scald his mouth, giving him another moment to contemplate that he had indeed left her and their house and their school.

"Yes, where I lived in Kansas City."

The air was getting colder and the smell of snow began to fill the air, yet he didn't want to go back into the warmth of the house. Sitting with his sister on the porch seemed to be warming him enough.

Madison took a sip of her hot chocolate and slurped up a marshmallow. She chewed on it then licked the chocolate from her lips.

"Did you live with that woman?"

Thomas shifted his eyes to the girl sitting beside him. Her hair was spun gold, just like Sarah's, but cut shorter.

She had small hoops in her ears, something his father would never allow Sarah to do. It was hard for him to remember that this was Madison and not Sarah. They were uniquely different, and that was wonderful.

"I lived in her house. It was a boarding house once. Do you know what that is?" Madison nodded. "Her grandmother lived there from the time she was a little girl until a few weeks back. Now Carissa lives there."

"And so do you?"

"Well…" He didn't have an answer for her so he sipped the hot chocolate again.

"Will you bring her back again to meet my dad?" Her eyes settled on him with a gentleness that made him want to gather her up and hold her tight to protect her from the world beyond her front door.

"Do you think he'd like to meet her?"

She nodded. "I think she's pretty."

"I think she's pretty, too."

"Are you going to marry her?"

He'd forgotten how inquisitive an eleven-year-old could be. "Things are very complicated between us." She sat close enough to him now that he could smell the fruity fragrance of her shampoo when the breeze caught it. It squeezed at his heart, just as it had when Hope had looked up to Carissa.

He'd missed long talks with Sarah, and though he realized she and Madison were very different, it still gave him solace to remember the joy in it. He'd forgotten that family could be a comfort.

Madison sat quietly and watched him with her big, blue eyes, as though studying him.

"Do you know how to play chess?"

The change in conversation had him laughing aloud. "Yes. I know how to play chess."

"Want to go in and play? We have a chess set made out of Disney characters." Her eyes were wide, and she was already on her feet, holding out her hand for him to take.

He looked at her open hand and felt a rush of emotion that he couldn't pin down. He'd fought for his father's acceptance, and he'd fought for Pablo's and the ensemble's as well. Suddenly acceptance was all around him, and he didn't know that he could trust it. How could he trust that Madison would want him in her life as her brother, or his mother would want the man as her son and not the boy? And Carissa, how could he accept the possibility that she was in love with him?

Life didn't work like this. Not for him, anyway. There had to be long periods of proving yourself before you were accepted and taken in. Then again, what if they all decided they didn't want him, like Pablo had? What if they all wanted him out of their lives when they realized he was no good for them?

It would be easier to just run away from it all again and start new. Why he'd thought taking Sophia's offer was plausible he didn't know. Hurt came only from those who knew you best, and she'd known him better than most. Now he looked up into the eyes of his young sister, and she held out her hand to accept him. He swallowed hard. It was just a game of chess he was committing to. It was just another day he could spend and feel it all out.

He reached for her hand and gave her a nod. "Well, who could pass that up?"

Carissa looked out over the water. They'd been over the ocean now for three hours, and the farther she flew away from Kansas City, the more hollow inside she felt.

"You have a man on your mind." Pablo handed her a drink and then occupied the seat next to her.

"Guilty." She accepted the drink and set it on her tray.

"Ah, the last time I flew with Sophia, she sat next to me sobbing over your father. Damn him."

Carissa's head popped up. She looked into the gorgeous, chocolate eyes of Pablo DiAngelo, and he laughed. "She'd never stopped loving him. Oh, she cried over him, said she hated him. Once she wished him a plague." That made them both laugh. "But she loved him always."

Carissa nodded and sipped the drink he'd brought. She coughed when she realized it wasn't just orange juice. Pablo laughed. "I thought it would loosen you up."

"I guess so," she said, setting it back on the tray.

"Tell me about this man you love."

"How do you know I love him?" She didn't want to tell him who she was in love with. Thomas hadn't spoken of Pablo much, and when he did, the conversation seemed to have a hitch. She'd also seen Pablo's reaction when her mother had mentioned Thomas's name.

"I know." He patted her hand. "It wears on your face."

"Well, I was wrong. I thought I could love him, but he doesn't love me. I don't think he knows how to love anyone."

"Ah, I know a man like this." He nodded and took her hand in his. "That man was me." He rested his head against the back of the seat. "I loved a man so much I would have died for him. He completed me in every way. However, I wouldn't admit it beyond the small circle of people I kept close. I'm not sure I admitted it to them either, but I was more at ease around them."

He turned his head to look at her. "I used Sophia mercilessly."

"Used her?" She'd never heard Sophia say such things.

"Yes. I kept her close to me so the world would think I was in love with her, and he'd walk behind us. Always behind us." He shook his head. "But it was him I loved."

"What happened?"

"Oh, we fought. He'd leave. I'd apologize, and we'd make up. He wanted me to tell the world I loved him, but I was too afraid to risk it. What if the world stopped loving me? I was wrong."

Pablo sucked in a breath and continued, "The night your mother decided to return to you and your father was the night the Vatican decided we were not worthy of their audience. He got into a fight with a paparazzo and ended up in the hospital." He took a sip of the drink he held in his other hand. "I swore to him that if he got out of that bed, I'd walk right out in front of the press and kiss him and profess my love."

"And I remember, that's what you did." It had been in the papers, and she'd seen it. He'd made his statement.

Pablo nodded. "I should have done it from the moment I told him I loved him. I shouldn't have waited until someone attacked him." He sat silently for a moment, looking past her and out the window. Then he focused back on her. "It wasn't easy for us after the Vatican canceled us and the world learned that I loved a man and had never had a relationship with Sophia. We all fought to keep our careers on track. The ensemble wasn't important to me anymore. I needed to understand what was happening in my life, but there were others in the ensemble to think about. My career was fine, but Pierre wanted to only be at home and wait for me to return. I agreed to that." His eyes were getting darker, and the lines around his lips tightened. "Then he was almost taken from me by someone I trusted and helped." He shook his head as if to ward off the tears that had started to form in his eyes.

"He's almost blind now because of the stupidity of another…"

"I'm so sorry," she said, softly laying her other hand on his arm.

"Oh, I'm the only one who cries about it. Pierre wears it like a badge of honor. Says that he was in that car by his own choice and it was as much his fault as that buffoon's who landed him in the hospital. Blames the wet streets of Paris."

He raked his fingers though his hair and let out a sigh. "Well, I still love him, and I would shout it if I needed to." He turned his head toward Carissa. "You'll be back soon. You tell this man you love that you love him, again, and maybe this time he'll listen."

"He doesn't even know I'm gone." She shifted her attention out the window.

Madison beat Thomas at chess four times before her father made her head upstairs and clean her room.

Parker Bennett sat down at the table, in the seat that his daughter had occupied, and rearranged the chess pieces back into place. Thomas hoped he didn't want to play. His mind certainly wasn't into it.

"Jane says you'll be leaving soon."

"I thought I'd head back in the morning." He guessed that since Parker was his mother's husband, that made him his father. He squirmed in his chair and then finally sat back in it fully.

"Well, I know Jane has made it perfectly clear, but you are family. You're welcome in our home anytime." Parker lifted his eyes toward Thomas, and he saw the sincerity in them. That was something he'd never seen in his own father's eyes.

"I appreciate that. I really do." He smiled as Parker sat back, draping his arm over the back of the chair, and looked at Thomas.

"She's missed you. I almost couldn't convince her to marry me because she missed you so much."

"I'm sorry. I didn't…"

Parker's hand rose, cutting off his apology. "I've known your mother a long time. She's never been happier than she has been with you here. She worried about you. She knew you were hurt."

Thomas shifted in his chair again as Parker leaned forward and rested his arms on the table.

"Will you be going back to—I'm sorry. I've forgotten her name." Parker's silver eyebrows furrowed.

"Carissa," he said on a sigh.

"Yes, Carissa."

Thomas shook his head. "I'll go back, but I don't think she'll have me."

"Well, you could ask, couldn't you?" He stood and patted Thomas on the back as he passed by.

Everyone else seemed to have faith that she'd take him back. Why didn't he think it was possible?

He knew why. He'd done the one unthinkable thing that Carissa had assumed he'd do and he'd promised not to—he'd walked out. He'd left her after having told her he wouldn't. When he'd called his mother, he didn't even give a thought to telling Carissa he'd be back. Probably, he realized, because he wasn't sure he would be. He had taken all of his belongings, hadn't he?

A sinking feeling hit his stomach when he realized he had to go back. He'd made a commitment to Carissa's school of music. He'd made a commitment to the students that would come into the school that he would teach them what he knew so well. He'd made a commitment to Sophia.

Whether Carissa would still love him, that would be another area to explore, and after seeing what his mother had done with her life, perhaps it was worth trying. After all, if everyone else saw good in him, maybe it was there. Maybe if he pushed away the thoughts that he was just like his father, they would go away.

Thomas sucked in a deep breath. If Carissa still loved him, maybe it would be enough. Maybe just asking for forgiveness and honoring the commitment he'd made to her would be enough to start a new life—without having to run away.

It was time for Thomas to go. He'd packed his few things and sat alone on his childhood bed. He hadn't anticipated the rush of joy that came when he thought about his childhood, looking at all the things his mother had kept. She'd preserved something he'd thought he'd lost to bitterness and grief, but in actuality, there were good times, and that was all thanks to his mother.

"So you're ready to go?" She materialized at the door as though he had summoned her. He nodded, and she walked toward him and sat down next to him on the bed.

Thomas breathed her in, thankful that she'd happened upon him in the cemetery because he knew he'd never have made the trip otherwise.

"Madison invited me for Thanksgiving." He smiled as he looked into his mother's familiar eyes. They weren't young anymore, as they had been when he'd seen her laughing at him and Sarah playing that silly song before…

"Will you come?" Her voice shook and he knew she was on the verge of tears, but she was holding them back.

He looked away. "Yes, I'll be here."

Jane touched her son's cheek and directed his eyes back to hers. "Thomas, bring her back with you. We'd love to have her, too."

"I made a horrible mistake, Mom. I thought I couldn't love, but seeing what you've built after what was taken from you…"

"It wasn't easy, Thomas. It's not supposed to be. And letting you go now is one of the hardest things I've ever done." A tear fell, and she wiped it quickly away. "As a mother who has lost everything, I want to hold onto you like you're still my little boy and keep you in this room safe and happy. I want to start all over again and make sure nothing bad ever happens to you again. But I can't do that. You're not a little boy anymore. You're a man. You're a man venturing into something very big."

"What is that?"

"You're in love. Not one part of it is easy, but the reward of it is great." She reached into the pocket of her dress and pulled out a small black box. "Here."

"What's this?" He opened it and saw a wedding ring he'd seen once when he was a small boy.

"It was my mother's," she said, watching him examine the ring in its box. "I told Sarah I would give it to her, but under the circumstances, I think you should give it to Carissa."

He was a grown man, but the sentiment brought tears to his eyes and he couldn't help shedding them. "Mom, I…"

"Love her more than you can admit. You want to keep her forever and make her happy."

The tears that had welled in his eyes blurred his vision. She was right. He wanted Carissa forever. He wanted to make her happier than she'd ever been. She wanted her school, her career, a marriage, and four children. And he wanted to be the man who fulfilled those dreams with her.

"Thank you." He kissed his mother on the cheek. "If she says yes, we'll both be here for Thanksgiving."

"We have a lot of time, Thomas. A lot of time to make up for the time we lost."

He was glad to hear her say that. Sixteen years was a long time, but it didn't have to be forever. Things could change. People could change. He'd finally seen it with his own eyes. You could move on from where you'd come from. Carissa had. His mother had. It was time for him to become who he wanted to be—and he wanted to be more than Carissa's lover. He wanted to be her husband.

Carissa had heard about Pablo DiAngelo's temper. Sophia had never kept that a secret. However, his anger today wasn't directed toward her; it was just the way he worked. The demeaning tension he caused in every musician either broke them or forced them to dig deeper and find the notes that would sound like angels singing— or, when necessary, demons and their destruction.

His wrath was worse if a note was missed or a musician didn't know the music.

She knew her material, from years of practice inspired by admiration for Pablo DiAngelo and her mother. She'd learned every song Pablo's ensemble had ever played so that she could play with Sophia, and they had done so routinely for eight years.

Pablo's tantrums had the pianist in tears. His timing was off, or his entrance was too slow.

Had he done that to Thomas? Had this been why Thomas didn't speak about his time with Pablo often?

The flutist yelled in Russian, the violinist didn't speak Italian, and Pablo's partner had an opinion on everything Pablo said.

She sat among them, the ensemble that Pablo DiAngelo had handpicked, in the rehearsal hall and wondered how her mother had endured such torture for ten years. Had it been different because they had all toured together for so long? Were they a family, unlike the ensemble that she played with that had been recently put together?

The thoughts weren't important when she thought about the opportunity that lay ahead. She'd never have had the chance to play for an international audience. In truth, she'd never taken the chance. She'd holed herself up in her house, taking care of Millie and Katie so that she'd never have to put herself on the line for rejection.

And just as the violinist's bow hit a note that made the entire ensemble stop and Pablo rise from his seat, throwing music in the air, she realized it had been that rejection that she'd always feared. It had stopped her from ever dreaming of grander things because what if she'd failed?

Carissa straightened her back as Pablo called for them to start from the beginning. That's what she needed. A new beginning for herself. A new start to her life where she wasn't afraid of rejection, but saw it as a new challenge.

It was time for her to shine.

She pulled her bow across the strings, thinking of what a wonderful opportunity it would be for her and for the school. She and Thomas could showcase their accomplishments in Rome under the tutelage of Pablo DiAngelo. She finished the song with a note of pure beauty that had Pablo beaming at her, and she herself feeling dizzy from the excitement of bigger and better things. The thought warmed her throughout, but then when it settled, it stung.

Thomas wasn't part of her dreams anymore. She had to remember that. Their relationship was like a cord that was played flat.

He'd walked out on her like others before him. He'd promised he wouldn't, but he had. He was just another piece of music she had memorized and never performed.

She took a deep breath and looked at her music as Pablo moved into position after yet another argument with Pierre. It was time for her to play. It was time for her to shine. And dammit, when she returned to the States, it was her time to move on.

The air in the car felt thick as Thomas tried to suck in as much of it as he could to calm his nerves. It wasn't working.

He'd parked out front of the school, but Carissa's car wasn't there. Perhaps she'd parked out back.

His palms were damp, his heart raced, and his head spun. He'd never been so nervous in his entire life. He reached across the car and grabbed the bouquet of flowers that sat on the passenger seat. Balancing the flowers in the crook of his arm, he raked his fingers through his hair, climbed out of the rental car, and closed the door with his hip.

There was a bell on the front door of the school now. It rang as the door shut behind him.

"Thomas!" Sophia's eyes grew wide with her smile as she approached him from the back. "You came back."

"Yes." It was all he could say because the sinking feeling in his gut was that he should have taken Carissa with him to meet his family. It shouldn't have been just him walking through that door. It should have been them. She should have been part of that joyous occasion, but he'd left her out—left her just as she'd feared he would. The thought made him dizzy.

He tried to refocus by taking in the new look of the school. It had come together in the short amount of time that he was gone. Walls were up, and the floor was finished. The rooms had doors. Carissa had to be so proud.

Sophia hugged him. "Did you bring me flowers?"

Thomas looked down at the flowers still in the crook of his arm, which Sophia had pressed between them when she'd hugged him. He'd nearly forgotten he was holding them, but he was grateful he had them. They hid his shaking hands.

Sophia was staring up at him, studying him the way a dear friend did when she knew something was wrong.

She laughed. "Thomas, I'm kidding. I know they're not for me. Is everything okay?"

"Yeah, um, is Carissa here?" He looked down the hall Sophia had come from. "Maybe you could just give these to her. I'm sure she doesn't want to see me." He pushed the flowers toward her, but she didn't take them. The concern in her eyes made guilt twist his stomach.

"Are you okay?" She reached for his arm.

"No. I'm not okay. I messed everything up, and I know she's going to kick me to the curb."

"Then you don't know my daughter very well at all." She took him by the arm and sat him down in one of the chairs in the parents' area. "I'm going to get you some water."

"I'm really not thirsty. I should go." He started to stand, but Sophia placed her hand on his shoulder.

"Sit. Take some deep breaths. I'll be back in a minute."

Sophia walked to the back of the school, where she would get Thomas a glass of water, but also where she could speak with her husband. David stood on a ladder, hanging the last of the shelves Carissa had asked him to put up while she was gone.

"Delivery?" He looked down at her.

"Of sorts." She filled the glass and turned to him with a smile. "He came back," she whispered.

"Who? The delivery man?"

"No." She laughed. "Thomas."

David shot down the ladder, his brows furrowed and his lips pursed. Sophia reached for his arm, and he stopped.

"If you need me—"

"I know." She smiled to let him know she understood his protective instincts and then started back toward the parents' area. David fell back and waited.

"Here," she said, handing Thomas the glass. His hand shook as he took it, and she tucked her lips between her teeth to keep her excitement from surfacing.

Thomas sipped at the water and then let out a breath. "Thank you."

"Now, do you want to tell me where you've been?" She raised her eyebrows and waited for his answer.

"I went home."

"To your family?" Her voice now shook, and she sat down next to him and inched her chair closer to him. "You saw your family?"

He took another sip of water. "I've been staying with my mother for the past few days. Her and her husband and their daughter."

"You have a sister?" Her tone softened, and she reached for his hand.

Thomas nodded. "She's the spitting image of Sarah. Her name is Madison."

"Oh, Thomas." She covered her mouth to stop the sob that tightened in her chest and moved up through her throat. It threatened to burst out when she thought of him having a family. His family.

"Anyway, I thought if my mother could piece her life back together, so could I." He reached into his pocket and pulled out a small, black box. He handed it to Sophia. "My mother gave me this to give to Carissa. I want to be more than just a teacher in her school, Sophia. I want to put my life back together, and I want her to be part of it."

She opened it, and the tears she'd held back released.

"Are you asking my wife to marry you?" David stood just beyond them watching.

"Oh, no sir." Thomas shot out of his seat.

"I'm kidding, Thomas." He stood next to his wife and looked down at the antique setting in her hand. "What is this?"

"It was my grandmother's wedding set. I'd like to give it to Carissa and ask her to marry me."

David ran his tongue over his teeth and studied Thomas. He nodded. "And you want my blessing?"

"It sure would make things smoother if I had it. I'm not sure I'll even have Carissa's blessing."

"I'm not sure you will either."

"David." Sophia looked up at him then back to Thomas. "I've known you for a long time, Thomas. I think Carissa would be lucky to have you."

"Thank you." He shifted his eyes to David. "Would it be okay if I asked your daughter to marry me?"

"You planned to do that anyway, didn't you?"

"Well, yes, I did, but…"

"Well, when you do, you can tell her you have my blessing."

"Well, I guess there is only one more person to ask."

Sophia exchanged a concerned look with David, well aware that Thomas knew something was wrong.

Thomas cleared his throat. "Where is Carissa?"

Chapter Thirteen

Carissa stood in front of the mirror in her dressing room. The dress Pablo had chosen for her was exquisite. She'd never looked so beautiful. He'd sent her roses. Beautiful, long-stemmed, red buds that felt like silk under her fingertips as she lifted one to her nose to smell its fragrance. He'd made it clear he wouldn't see her and the other members of the ensemble until moments before they stood together to perform.

When the door opened, she looked up to see Pierre slowly make his way into the room, his eyes shielded by dark glasses, his hands extended to help lead him to her.

"Ah, I smell the sweet perfume of roses."

Carissa stood and moved to him. His extended hands were an invitation for her to take them so he could embrace her, and he pulled her into his arms.

"He will never tell you, so I thought I would. He couldn't have been more pleased that you came with him. He really wanted Sophia, but he thinks you are as talented, if not more so," he added, moving back from her as though to study her face. "But I will deny that if you repeat it."

"I wouldn't dream of it," she said, smiling at her new friend.

The door opened again, and to her surprise, Sophia stuck her head around the door. Pride swelled in Carissa's chest. Her mother had refused the invitation to play the venue she'd lost, choosing her role as a wife and mother over restarting her career, but she'd come to share it with her.

"Mom!" She let go of Pierre's hands and ran to her mother's waiting arms. "You're here."

"I wouldn't have missed it for the world. After all, you took my place," she teased.

"Is that my beauty?" Pierre turned and waited for Sophia to come to him.

"Pierre, oh Pierre." She went to him, his arms open to her. "I've missed you so much."

"Enough to have visited me in the past eight years?" he asked with a straight face.

Sophia sighed and bowed her head.

"I'm kidding, my beauty. You got the man you loved, the most talented daughter, and had a baby waiting for you when you got home. Oh, Sophia, what a wonderful life you've been given."

"It has been wonderful. It has." She gave Carissa a grand smile then she turned her attention back to Pierre. "What about you? Pablo told me you'd been in an accident. I didn't know about it. I'm so sorry."

He shook his head. "Oh, he blames…well, it's not important. Truth is, we'd had too many drinks, the streets were slick, and the press was after us. I hate that press. We were trying to outrun them. It wasn't his fault. Pablo did what he could to shift the attention of the press away from us. I'm not surprised you didn't hear."

"Your sight?"

"It's going. It's going quickly, but my ears are fine. And I hear music, I don't see it."

Sophia kissed him on the cheek. "You are still amazing. Do you know that?"

"Of course I do." He laughed.

"Well, I'd better get to my seat," she said, turning back toward Carissa.

Carissa took her mother's hands in hers. "Dad?"

"He's here, and so is Hope. Pablo pulled some strings," she admitted.

"I'm so happy he did. This is the best surprise ever." She kissed her mother's cheeks. "I'm going to do my best. This is so much more than first chair. This really should be you."

"No, it was meant to be for you." She touched Carissa's face. "We'll meet you back at the hotel when you're done. I'm sure the evening will only get better." She kissed her daughter and left the room.

Pierre excused himself, and Carissa sat alone.

She held her cello between her legs, leaning into the instrument, holding it against her like a child needing to be comforted. She ran her fingers over the strings running the first song through her mind. When the door opened again, Pablo walked through in his black tuxedo.

She rose to him, surprised that he would have stepped into her room after having made it perfectly clear he would not see his ensemble.

She could see why the world loved him. Aside from his beautiful voice, he was, simply put, one of the most gorgeous men to walk the planet. His dark, mysterious looks, his deep chocolate eyes, and the build of a god. He was pure pleasure on the eyes.

"Bella, are you ready to make history."

"I'm sick," she said with a hand on her stomach, and that caused him to laugh.

"Your mother threw up on my shoes once. You will not."

"No, I will not." She stood and held the neck of the instrument. "Thank you for bringing my family."

"My pleasure." He took her hand and kissed it. "Sophia had to be here, even if she didn't play."

"I really appreciate it."

"They will come for your cello in a moment. You will meet me down the hall with the rest in five minutes," he instructed, and she nodded.

Pablo kissed each of her cheeks. "You've been quite an asset to my ensemble. I would like you to think about giving up your school and staying in Rome."

"Pablo, I don't know what to say. I—"

"You say nothing. You think about it." He turned and strode out of the room.

A few moments later, a young man came for her cello, to set it on stage, and she met the ensemble down the hall as instructed. Pierre gathered with them while Pablo finished his preparations.

"As soon as this evening is over, we will be escorted by car to the hotel. You will change and have one hour before Pablo expects you for celebration drinks."

They all nodded as the instructions were given. There wasn't a member of the ensemble that didn't fully understand the impact of what was about to happen.

Carissa stood at the edge of the stage with the others. The pianist wiggled his fingers, warming them up. The violinist's head swayed back and forth, her eyes closed, and Carissa knew she heard music in her mind. The flutist fixed his shirt cuffs.

She knew they all had their own ways of preparing for their performance. She, however, couldn't move past the sounds around her.

The murmur of the crowd, speaking in Italian, resonated through the theater. Not one voice more dominant than the other. The many conversations blended together in their own symphony.

A man in red robes passed by them and out to the stage. She heard his shoes click on the stage, and the audience quieted down.

The sickness in her stomach rose into her throat, and she closed her eyes and breathed deeply as the man onstage welcomed the audience and introduced the pope.

Carissa's eyes shot open, and the quick glances between the members of the ensemble made her realize that each of them was as panicked as she was. The pope had summoned them to play for him, and he was there to listen.

The lights went down, and the ensemble took their positions on the stage. The lighting cued, and Carissa raised her bow. Pablo's voice rang through the hall and history began.

Only one thing was missing from the most momentous night of her life—and that was Thomas.

The raw nerves that had made her sick drove her through the performance, but the silent breaking of her heart was sure to drive her mad.

The concert was over. Carissa sat in the limousine with the others, and after a few seconds hubbub, they all fell silent. Every eye was wide. Every mouth wore a smile. The air was full of electricity. But though they all felt the music, there were no words that could be shared among those who didn't speak the same language.

They parted ways in the hotel, going to their rooms to prepare for the upcoming celebration. One hour wasn't quite enough time to get the excitement out of Carissa's body. Before she changed her dress, she'd need to scream into a pillow. Energy was pulsing through her. She'd played the Vatican. She'd met the pope. She'd lived out her mother's dream.

Juggling the roses that Pablo had given her, she slid the key to her door into the reader then pushed it open. She stopped in the doorway, and the giddy smile that had been on her lips vanished. Her eyes opened wide when she noticed the lights were on and dimmed. Champagne chilled in a bucket on the table. Two flutes sat near the bucket. A vase of roses sat on the end table by the sofa. As the door closed behind her, she noticed the coat.

Thomas's coat.

Her breath whooshed out of her lungs. She felt the blood drain from her face, and her head spun.

"You were amazing tonight." His voice carried through the suite.

Carissa turned to see him observing her from the doorway to the bedroom.

"You were there?"

"It was the biggest venue any of us could have dreamed about. You fulfilled that dream, Carissa. You were amazing." He smiled as he walked cautiously toward her.

Emotions ran through her so quickly that she wasn't sure which she was supposed to express.

He was here. He was in Rome. He was in her room with champagne and roses. He'd been at the Vatican. He'd come to hear her play.

He'd left her.

It seemed that anger won over joy. Her jaw tightened, and her lips pursed. "Why are you here?" She snapped out the question and watched as his eyes widened.

"I needed to talk to you."

"Now? You need me now?" She turned and set the roses Pablo had given her on the large, mahogany table behind her. "You should go."

"You should hear me out."

She didn't speak. She was too stunned to speak.

He moved to the sofa and gestured with his hand for her to join him. "Why don't you sit down?"

"Why don't you go to hell, Thomas?"

"Well, I see this is going to be an interesting evening." He ran his tongue over his teeth. "Fine," he said as he walked to the champagne and opened it. He poured her flute full and handed it to her, and then filled the other for himself.

"If this was supposed to be a celebration…"

"Well, let's just say we might as well get drunk first." He lifted the flute to his lips, but she shot her hand up between them and pulled his from his lips. It tore at her to watch him even dare to drink.

"Don't. Don't drink it."

"Why not?"

"You don't drink." She kept her voice soft. "There is no need for you to ruin your sobriety over my success." She lowered her voice further. "Or my stubbornness."

He smiled. "Well then, why don't you sit and sip champagne, and I'll do the talking I wanted to do."

Carissa nodded, feeling a heavy burden in her chest. She'd never have been able to live with herself had she thought Thomas had begun drinking again because of her. She took his flute in her other hand and sat down on the cold, leather sofa.

With both hands filled with glasses, she stared up at him as he paced before her with his hands in the pockets of his slacks. She noticed that he again reminded her of Jimmy Stewart as he rubbed his chin and then ran his fingers through his hair, which once again was too long and absolutely stunning on him, she thought.

"I went home."

"Home?"

"Yeah. When I left, I went back to my mother's house and stayed for a few days." His eyes lifted to hers, and she smiled.

"That's wonderful." Her voice was even. The smile was genuine. She wasn't angry at that very moment. She was happy for him.

"It was great. I spent time with my sister. We played chess, had hot chocolate, and I told her stories of Sarah when she asked me to."

"Oh, Thomas…"

"I slept in my bed," he added. "She kept my bed and all my things. It was truly like going home. Only this time, I felt safe. Really safe." He shifted his eyes to her. "Like I do when I sleep in your arms."

Carissa set the flutes down on the table. Then she picked hers back up. She drank down the bubbling liquid inside and felt it rush to her head.

He was watching her when she looked back up at him. His eyes searched her face. "I'm not my father, Carissa." The words were a bold statement, and Carissa could only stare at him, taking in what he said. "I've lived a great life. I've made a lot of mistakes, but they don't have to dictate what comes next."

"No, they don't," she agreed. She set down her flute and stood. "Thomas, you are a wonderful man. You are talented and caring. I never would have told you I love you if I didn't think so."

He walked around the coffee table and gathered her hands in his.

"They want us to come out for Thanksgiving. They'd like to meet you and get to know you."

"Really?"

"Yes."

"Why?"

"They want to get to know the woman I love." His eyes settled into hers. Her mouth dropped open, and she gasped. "Yes, Carissa, I'm saying I love you."

"Thomas…"

"Do you want me to say it again? I love you."

Her mouth opened even wider as her eyebrows drew together.

"I'll say it again. I love you, Carissa Kendal. I love you. I love you. I love you."

"Oh, God!" Tears were threatening to surface. Her lip began to quiver, and she bit it and just stared at him.

"I love you. I want you to be my wife and have at least four kids with me."

"Really?"

"Are you trying to make this harder for me?" he laughed.

The knock at the door halted her answer. She kept her eyes focused on him as she answered. Her father stood beyond the threshold.

"Well, is my baby girl engaged?" David gathered her in his arms and kissed her cheeks.

"Not yet," Thomas answered. "She doesn't seem to be able to give me an answer."

"You knew?" Carissa looked up at David and Sophia, who followed with Hope right alongside her.

"Of course I knew." David stiffened his shoulders and gave a nod in Thomas's direction. "He's a gentleman. He asked me first."

"You asked my father for his blessing?" She turned toward Thomas. Her wide-eyed stare met his smiling eyes as he nodded.

"Yes. And he gave it to me."

"What is all of this?" Pablo's voice boomed from behind them. "Where is my star?" He pushed his way past Carissa's family and walked to her. He gathered her in his arms and kissed her on the lips. "I came first to you. I wanted to tell you how wonderful you were."

Carissa's hands rested on his arms and she smiled as Pierre walked in behind him.

"Pablo, thank you. It was a wonderful and…" Her words stopped when Pablo lifted his head and his focus shifted over her shoulder.

"What the hell is he doing here?" He let go of Carissa, pushing her to the side, and rushed across the room toward Thomas, his eyes full of fury and his step quick and swift.

Thomas stepped back as Pablo knocked over a chair, barreling his way toward him.

His hand came up in a fist. Carissa watched in horror as Pablo swung. She screamed Thomas's name as Thomas ducked the first punch and gave Pablo a shove. Pablo's left hand hooked in front of him and connected with Thomas's jaw.

Thomas flew into the wall and down to the floor. Pablo jumped on top of him and drove his fist into Thomas's face again and again until she and David could pull him back.

"What is wrong with you?" she screamed at Pablo as she knelt down next to the man she loved.

Pierre moved next to David, who held Pablo at bay. Pablo shook off David's hold.

"God dammit! What is that son of a bitch doing here? I told you never to come back!"

Pierre touched his arm. "Stop. Pablo, stop!"

"He almost kills you and you want me to stop?" His voice was filled with fury. "You bastard! I'm going to kill you."

"Get out!" Carissa stood and glared at Pablo.

"You're involved with him?" Pablo pushed a wild lock of hair from his eyes. "This is the man you love?"

"Yes. This is the man I love and I'm going to marry." She heard Thomas moan behind her, and she returned to his side. She lifted his head into her arms. His cheek and lip were split and bleeding. Already his eye was swelling shut and blood trickled down his face. "God, Thomas, are you all right?"

He only nodded.

Pierre shouted at Pablo, "You are such an idiot! Why must you do things like this? You ruined his career. Isn't that enough?"

"Enough for almost losing you?"

"It wasn't his fault," he said as though he were repeating it for the millionth time.

"He drove that car right into a barrier. Look at you. You can't see. You walk with a limp. You were almost dead."

"I'm not dead. I'm here. I hear what you are saying. I feel your anger. But you have to believe me if you love me." Pierre's words cracked with tears.

Thomas tried to sit up. "Pierre, don't."

"No. If he wants to ruin lives over it, then he will ruin mine. Thomas was only helping me."

"Helping? Driving you while he was drunk?"

"Yes." Pierre took a deep breath. "I was with another man."

The room fell silent. Pablo stared at Pierre in disbelief. He scrubbed his hands over his face. Pierre moved closer to him, his hands reached out to feel for him.

"It was a mistake. I met up with him. We had a few drinks." He threw his hands in the air. "We had a lot of drinks. Thomas happened to be there. And he happened to have had too many already before he spotted me. He took me aside and promised he wouldn't say anything, but he thought we should go."

"Pierre, you don't have to—"

Pierre held up a hand to Thomas to stop him.

"The man I was meeting thought I was hooking up with Thomas. He threatened us. We got in my car and started out. Thomas was in better shape than I was. I didn't realize he was drunk. Then the press was coming after us. The guy was setting me up to get to you, to expose you. We were outrunning them, the roads were slick, and he lost control of the car." He began to weep.

Thomas's head fell back into Carissa's arms. Tears fell from her eyes, and Thomas lifted his hand to brush them from her cheeks.

Pablo stood silent. The room was still, and all eyes were on him as he turned toward Thomas.

"You covered for him? You took the fall so I wouldn't know he was cheating on me?"

Thomas shifted his head to look at Pierre. Pierre nodded, and Thomas swallowed hard. "I did what I thought was right by my friend."

"I killed your career." Pablo's voice shook as he spoke.

Thomas's jaw hardened. He blinked once.

Pablo's shoulders bowed. "You have nothing."

"I have Carissa. She's all I need." Carissa took his hand and gave it a squeeze.

Pablo's eyes tightened. He lifted his chin, turning toward Pierre. "You are not the man I thought you were."

"I've lived my life walking two steps behind you. One night I decided to walk on my own and look where it got me."

"One night? You expect me to believe that you've done this only once?"

Pierre lifted his hand toward Pablo and reached until he touched him. "I expect you to believe that I made an error in judgment only once. I expect that you remember that Thomas was there, drunk perhaps, yet levelheaded enough to steer me out of the arms of a man only wishing to do us both harm. And," he continued, "I expect you to, yes, believe that it was a one-time thing. I have never…" His words broke off as Sophia walked to him, placing her hands on his arms.

Carissa watched as Pablo stood and surveyed the room. He looked at Thomas lying in her arms. She reached for a tissue on the end table and wiped a trickle of red from his cheek that Pablo had bloodied in his anger.

Pablo sighed and scrubbed his hands over his face.

"I pushed Pierre to the back in order to remain in the spotlight. I used you, Sophia, to keep my secrets," he said, turning to her then back toward Thomas. "And I worked very hard to ruin your career and leave you with nothing."

He walked toward Thomas and Carissa. She winced as he knelt down next to them.

Pablo focused his eyes on them. "Forgiveness is a hard thing to ask for," he said softly.

"Yes, and it's a hard thing to give." Thomas moved from Carissa's protective arms and sat up as straight as he could. "But in the past few weeks, I've learned a lot about forgiving."

Pablo gently placed a hand on each of their shoulders.

"I'm asking for your forgiveness now."

"And I forgive you." Thomas tried to smile, but winced in pain. He leaned back in Carissa's arm, and she dabbed his lip with the tissue then kissed the top of his head.

She wanted everyone to leave so she could take care of him and love away his pains. All of his pains.

Pablo still knelt next to them. "Dear, God, look at what I've done to you. You need a doctor." Pablo reached for his arm to help him to his feet, but Thomas shook his head.

"I have Carissa. She'll take good care of me."

Carissa laid a kiss on his forehead. "I promise."

"I heard you tell this lunatic you were going to marry me."

She laughed through the tears. "You heard that?"

"Yeah. I thought I should confirm it."

Carissa nodded. "Mr. Thomas Samuel, I'd love to be your wife."

Epilogue

Spring was all around Katie, and she drank it in. The trees had new leaves, a promise of hope. The heads of tulips had rose from the ground and colored the many flower boxes that Katie and her own mother had planted so many times when she was a young girl.

She looked out over the backyard where she'd played as a child, and she smiled. She'd married her George in that yard, and her son had married his wife there. When Sophia and David had finally made it to the altar, they too married in the beautiful yard.

Once again, Katie sat among her flowers and her family and watched as two people who loved one another became man and wife.

The students from their school of music played the "Wedding March" with their chosen instruments as Carissa walked down the aisle. The mixed sounds from the instruments might have been as welcoming as fingernails on a chalkboard to most, but to Thomas and Carissa, it was more beautiful than any symphony, and that fact shone in their smiles.

Carissa's father gave her a smile as he lifted her veil, and Katie watched as the big man wiped tears from his eyes.

Sophia took Katie's hand and gave it a squeeze.

"I did okay, didn't I, Grandma?" Sophia whispered as the minister began the ceremony. "I learned my matchmaking from the best."

Katie smiled. Yes, Sophia had learned from the best. At least Carissa and Thomas had had the foresight to get married right away. Sophia and David had dragged out their courtship for over a decade, making her and her best friend wait to see that their matchmaking had paired the perfect couple.

Hope turned from her sister's side and waved at her mother and great-grandmother. Katie waved back. Someday it would be her turn to wed in the beautiful yard. It pained Katie to think she wouldn't be there to see it, but she'd be there in spirit. Who knew, maybe she'd be there in some small way to play matchmaker for Hope too. After all, she'd already written letters to people in Mandy's past to let them know Hope existed. Katie knew that there would come a time when Hope would want to know where she came from. And a time when her family—her whole family—would welcome her into their hearts.

It gave Katie some solace to know that, though she couldn't hand pick a man for Hope, perhaps she'd set into motion all the pieces for Hope's discovering where she came from and realizing just how blessed she was to have David and Sophia for her parents. It was a matchmaking of sorts, Katie thought.

Someday love would come looking for Hope too, and Katie smiled thinking that she just might be a part of that

I hope you enjoyed Encore, book two in the Matchmaker Series. Please indulge in the first chapter of Finding Hope, book three in the series, releasing August 1, 2013.

Finding Hope

Chapter One

He'd seen it all in his chosen profession. The most popular: the cheating husband. There were bosses who suspected employees were skimming the till. And like the angry wives', the bosses' suspicions were usually correct. A missing relative or child was just as common, but this case piqued his interest more than most.

Trevor Jacobs looked down at the manila folder on the passenger seat of his car. He tugged at his collar. The Missouri summer was warming the inside of his car to temperatures that he was sure would kill a man. He picked up the folder and flipped it open.

Finding Mandy Marlow had been a challenge because she'd disappeared when she was seventeen. That had been forty years ago.

The last time her mother had seen her, Mandy'd had a newborn infant in her arms and had come back begging for money. Ruth Marlow, Mandy's mother, had given him the case's scant details over the phone. His notes clearly reflected that Mandy hadn't gone asking for a place to stay or for help with the baby. She had wanted ten thousand dollars and they had refused. She had told them she'd be living with friends. Friends who would love her and her baby, unlike her parents.

He'd finally tied Mandy to a David Kendal, a retired airline pilot living in Kansas City, Missouri.

Mandy Marlow had lived in the Kansas City area approximately seven years after she had left her parents' house. Her DMV records showed she'd lived in a house owned by David Kendal and exactly seventeen years after she'd last been seen by her family she changed her name to

Mandy Kendal. He'd searched marriage records, but he found no record that Mandy and David had actually been married. She had assumed the name through proper channels. However, their names did appear together on the birth certificates of Carissa Marlow Kendal and one Hope Katherine Kendal.

Hope Kendal had been born by cesarean moments after they had pronounced Mandy Kendal dead. She had died of heart failure and had papers that had strictly instructed that she not be revived.

She hadn't been.

David Kendal married a Sophia Burkhalter only three weeks later. He flipped through the notes. "In a lovely back yard ceremony of the home of the bride's grandmother Katherine Burkhalter," the newspaper clipping had stated. Adoption records showed that Sophia, now Kendal, had adopted Carissa, then seventeen, and the newborn Hope only three months after she'd been born.

What a tidy package, he thought. Ex-lover of the dead woman shares custody of his children with his new wife. What a twisted novel plot that would make. He laughed. However, armed with the facts he had, he knew it had been that simple.

A change of heart, or perhaps a shove in that direction, had Mandy Marlow—Mandy *Kendal*—giving up her children and refusing to fight for her own life.

Sweat beaded on his brow. Trevor reached for his bottle of water. It had grown warm. He drank it down and tossed it into the backseat with the other bottles he'd discarded there. He knew he wasn't the ideal patron for a car rental company.

He flipped through his notes again and stared into the face he'd become familiar with.

Hope Katherine Kendal.

She stood in a crowded room, but the camera had zoomed in on her. She'd been intrigued by something, or someone. Long blonde hair cascaded behind her shoulders and crystal blue eyes watched him from the photo. She had lips that were full and just a bit pouty. The face that mesmerized from the photo had a cherubic look to her, but a super model's features.

He knew he'd been fascinated by it too long, too many times. He'd seen it in his dreams. He'd found himself driving down the road thinking about her face.

Trevor checked his watch. He'd been sitting in the cemetery, in his parked car, for over two hours. He'd wait another two hours and then he'd move on.

But he didn't have to wait any longer.

A blue Miata pulled up between him and the headstone that read Mandy Marlow Kendal. The beautiful blonde that he'd familiarized himself with stood there in person. He felt his heart race a little faster.

The pace of his heart was different from when he was about to confront most of those whom he'd followed. That was adrenaline. This was lust.

Hope stood just outside her car. She was dressed in jeans that rode low on curvy hips. She wore her tie-dyed shirt tucked in, giving her a look of being taller than she was. Her hair fell well down her back in a long tail.

Large sunglasses shielded her eyes, but he knew how blue they were.

She wasn't moving. He was far enough from her he knew she couldn't see him, but he wondered what she was thinking when she stood still on the narrow dirt road. She reached through the open window of her car and pulled out a bouquet of flowers.

Another car pulled up behind her. Trevor watched with intrigue. Carissa Kendal Samuel—he'd familiarized himself with her face as well—climbed out of her car and approached Hope.

He watched them exchange a few words and then an embrace. It was amazing how different sisters could be. Hope was fair. Her blonde hair was strikingly different from the dark hair of her sister. Carissa stood a few inches taller than Hope and her figure was straighter where Hope's was voluptuous.

Arm in arm the sisters walked toward the grave of their birth mother. A smile crossed Trevor's lips. Right on time.

Carissa laced her arm through her sister's. "So, in twenty-three years this is the first time I caught you here?"

"You knew I came every year on the day that she died." On the anniversary of her own birth.

"I did." Carissa rested her head against her sister's. "I just wasn't sure why you did."

"She's a piece of me. She's a piece I don't know. A piece I'm afraid to ask about."

"We've always been open about her."

"I know. But I'm old enough to really understand. I think I want to understand now." Hope bent and laid the flowers on Mandy's grave then stood erect next to her sister again. "Do you really think she was always the person you knew?"

Carissa snorted out a laugh. "I hadn't thought about it. My memories of her aren't the happiest ones. I guess I never gave any consideration to who she was aside from that."

Hope gave her sister a nod. Since she'd been ten years old she'd been curious. She'd remembered asking her father on the day they had buried her great-grandmother, Katie, if he'd take her to see her birth mother's grave. She'd whispered it in his ear, not wanting to hurt her mother's feelings. He'd agreed. They hadn't gone that day, but he'd taken her.

They had stood where she now stood with her sister on her arm. They'd looked down at the grave without a word. She hadn't asked questions and he hadn't offered anything either. They just stood together in awkward silence.

The woman in the grave was not her mother. She understood that. Yes, Mandy had given birth to her, but that wasn't motherhood. Sophia was her mother and would remain in her heart as just that. She'd raised her, molded her, and above all else loved her unconditionally. However, Mandy Marlow Kendal's blood ran through her veins, and unlike her sister, whose biological father raised them both, Hope knew nothing of the two people who'd given her life.

Carissa gave her a nudge.

"I have to get back to the school. Thomas is planning dinner for you tonight. You are coming, aren't you?"

"Me miss a birthday dinner that Thomas made? Not on your life." She kissed her sister's cheek. "Tell him I'll be there and I'll bring treats for the kids."

"No candy," Carissa pleaded. "Aiden has had enough sweets since he's been staying with Mom while we work. Bryce's teeth are going to rot out from under his braces, and Julie and Becky, well they just don't need it."

"Okay. I get it. I won't let you know." Hope grinned up at her sister, who only shook her head.

"You're as bad as Mom."

"We're entitled."

"Wait till you have kids. You will curse her and her giving ways."

"I'll take your word for it."

They fell silent again.

"Are you going to stay?" Carissa asked.

"Yeah. I think I need a few more minutes."

"I'll see you tonight, then." Hope nodded without looking up. "Happy birthday," Carissa added.

Hope tilted her head up toward her sister and smiled. "Thanks."

Carissa walked back to her car, leaving her sister to gather her thoughts over the grave of Mandy Kendal.

He watched Carissa's car drive away. Finally, he thought. He couldn't take the heat inside the car any longer.

Trevor slipped his business card into his pocket, climbed from the car, and put on his sunglasses. He walked across the grounds, slowly, as though he were searching for a stone.

She looked up at him as he neared and gave him a smile. Not an affectionate one, but that of someone who knew if you were in a cemetery, someone there mattered to you.

He wiped a hand over his brow.

"Hot day."

"Sure is." Her voice rang in his ears, penetrating every part of him. He'd studied the face, memorized the eyes, but had never heard the angelic ring of her voice.

A smile slid over his lips. "Visiting? Is this your grandmother?" He nodded to the grave where she stood.

"My birth mother."

Trevor nodded again. She was specific, he thought.

Hope scanned a look over him, and though her eyes were still shielded by the sunglasses, a knot twisted in his stomach because she was looking right at him. Those eyes he'd studied in the picture and dreamed of at night focused on him.

"Are you searching for someone?"

"Yeah. My aunt is here somewhere." At least he wasn't lying. It was his great-great-aunt. Her grave marker read the year 1877, but he didn't need to give the details. "I always forget where she's buried."

Hope nodded. "Good luck finding her."

She turned to walk back toward her car.

This was the point in his findings, in a case like this, where he would introduce himself and tell her why he'd been sent to find her. He wasn't ready for that. He wasn't ready to hand her his card and say, "Your birth father is looking for you." He wasn't ready to put away the feeling he had when her eyes looked in his direction.

"I'm Trevor," he called out to her and she stopped. "Trevor Jacobs."

Hope turned back to him. "It's nice to meet you." She smiled warmly and continued back to her car.

"And you are?" He followed, then slowed, realizing he appeared too anxious.

"Are you following me?" She tilted down her sunglasses. The piercing blue eyes he knew so well looked right into him, and his heart slammed in his chest. He could barely breathe.

"I'm just new to the area. You know, trying to meet anyone I can." He looked around. "Anywhere I can." He laughed and she pushed up her glasses and studied him.

"Hope Kendal." She extended her hand to him.

He took it and the shock that zapped between them had them both pulling their hands away.

"Wow," he whispered as he looked down at his hand then back up to her.

"Shocking," she joked. "Well, Mr. Jacobs, it was nice to meet you. I hope you find your aunt."

He couldn't move.

Hope walked to her car and he watched as she drove away. He looked back at his hand. It still tingled.

"It was a sign, Hope Kendal." He turned back toward his car with a wide smile. "And I believe in signs."

He swung open the car door and crawled in behind the wheel.

Hope watched him climb into his car from her rearview mirror. He headed out of the cemetery in the opposite direction. When she was sure he was out of sight, she stopped the car with a jolt and took a deep breath.

She rubbed her hand on her pant leg, trying to ease the tingling in it. She shook her head. She could hear her great-grandmother telling her she would meet a man someday that would take her breath away. They were walking through a meadow, she recalled.

Hope moved her head from side to side, trying to ease the tension in her neck. She was losing her mind. She'd never walked in the meadow with her great-grandmother. She'd only been ten when Katie died and she'd been too frail to walk anywhere.

But it was her voice that Hope heard in her vivid dreams. It was clear.

Hope adjusted behind the wheel, checked her mirrors, and put the car back into drive. She wasn't going to worry about her sanity. She was fine. Everyone had dreams that meant a lot. She, however, had them often.

Katie Burkhalter had been in her dreams since she'd been a small girl. She understood that. That was remembering someone you loved. As she'd gotten older, Katie was only a memory. There were no more dreams.

When she turned twenty the dreams had returned.

She and Katie walked in meadows, painted pictures of flowers, and even played the piano together. That thought alone had her laugh. She'd taken piano lessons from the time she was eight. Her brother-in-law had had the patience of a saint as he tried to teach her, but she was no good. The daughter of a world-renowned cellist and the sister of one of the most sought-after music teachers in the area, Hope Kendal couldn't keep rhythm or play to save her soul. She'd started on the piano and moved on to other instruments. It was no use. She was not a musician.

She was an artist.

Hope didn't hear the world, she saw it in vivid color and texture. What her mother, sister, and brother-in-law could convey in music, she could convey on canvas.

Luck had been on her side. The small store next to her sister's music school had become available when she'd turned twenty-one. Already established as a mural artist, she opened a small gift shop where she could also sell her paintings and work on them as well. Business wasn't booming, but it kept her busy, happy, and close to her family.

Now, with her hand still tingling and her grandmother's voice ringing in her ears, she felt the need to paint. She drove back to her studio.

She would keep the store closed for the rest of the day. After all, it was her birthday. She deserved a day off, but she would paint. She would paint him.

Music filtered through the walls as Hope set up her canvas and selected a pencil to sketch the face of the stranger she'd met. Thomas had a student just beyond the wall that separated Hope's studio area from the music school. She recognized the muffled song. How many times had he tried to get her to play it? How many times had he not given up? How many times had she tried it? She was seventeen before they all decided her talents lay in another form. Painting was her avenue of expression.

Of course, her perseverance in playing the piano had stemmed from her being enamored with her brother-in-law. She'd been eight when he'd walked into her life. Now he was the father of her two nieces and two nephews and still the light of her life. She knew how blessed she was to have two very stable and wonderful men in her life.

She began to block in the shading and planes of the face etched in her mind. The broad forehead accentuated by the short dark hair, the well-groomed brows that shadowed the deep-set, dark eyes, and the mouth... That mouth that housed a perfect set of white teeth behind perfect lips, which she was sure were soft, yet strong.

Hope lifted the pencil and looked down at the shadows on the white canvas. He stared up at her. She lifted her fingers to the canvas and felt the same shock travel through her fingers as she'd felt when he'd touched her.

Dear God, what was it about the man? Trevor Jacobs, she reminded herself, with his smile and his deep voice that still rang in her ears.

He'd happened upon her in a cemetery of all places. You didn't meet the man of your dreams in a cemetery.

She put down the pencil. The music from the school next door had stopped and she noticed that the light outside had dimmed. She'd been drawing the face of Trevor Jacobs for hours. She glanced down at her watch and decided she had just enough time to go home, shower, and change before she headed to her sister's house for dinner.

A smile slid across her lips. It was her birthday. Her twenty-third birthday to be exact, and she still loved blowing out candles and ripping into presents. Now it was even more fun. Her sister's children begged to help blow the candles, and little Becky, who had just turned six, was very fond of ripping paper off of gifts. It couldn't get any better than that.

Trevor watched the lights in the small apartment turn on as Hope walked from the door to the back, where he knew her bedroom must be. He hadn't actually gone through her apartment, but he'd studied her long enough. However, now that he'd spoken to her face-to-face he wasn't comfortable watching her. Before it had been to ensure that Hope Kendal was in fact the daughter of Mandy Marlow and his client, but now he sat in his car out in the street just because he wanted to be near her.

He tossed his head against the back of his seat. He'd never stopped from identifying himself when the time was right. His job had been to find a missing person. He'd done that. He'd found her buried in a cemetery in Kansas City, Missouri.

Once he'd found Mandy Marlow his job was to prove that she did indeed have a child that, by calculation, would be twenty-three years old. If in fact he found that there was a child, he was to contact his client and inform him of the findings. He'd done that. What a phone call that had been.

He'd told Donald Buchanan that he had found Mandy Marlow. The silence on the other end had been disturbing.

"How is she?" Donald had asked.

Trevor had frozen. Damn! The man hadn't known she was dead.

"Sir, she died twenty three years ago," he said cautiously and heard a sharp intake of breath on the other end of the line. There was more silence. "Sir, are you okay?"

"Yes. Yes." He cleared his throat. "I'm sorry. I guess I hoped that... well, it's not important."

"You were correct though. She did have a child that matches the age you gave me. In fact, she turned twenty-three today."

The silence on the other end of the line was different. He didn't hear deep breaths as he'd heard when he'd told him Mandy was dead. He was sure that if he could see Donald Buchanan, the man would be smiling.

"I knew it," he said simply. "You said she?"

"Yes, sir. A daughter." He was reluctant to give him her name. He still had half his fee to collect from the man, and he'd already finished what he'd been asked to do. Simply find Mandy Marlow and see if she had a child. He'd done that.

"Thank you."

"Just doing my job," he ensured him.

"I would like to meet with her, but my wife… she can't know about her."

"That will be up to you, sir. I can give her your contact information."

"No. She wouldn't know about me, would she?"

"Well she knew about Mandy, sir. She was at her grave today."

"Yes, but if Mandy died when she was so young, then she's been raised by another family, perhaps a family that has protected her from me all this time."

Trevor was sure of that.

Donald sighed into the phone.

"Can you spend more time there getting to know about them? I would like to know who they are and what they are like before I approach her."

"I'm not sure that's…"

"Please, Mr. Jacobs." He let out another sigh. "I've spent the past twenty-three years wishing I had found Mandy. I should never have let her disappear as I did. She was like that. She'd just disappear from your life. But I never forgot her." He was silent for a moment. "Mr. Jacobs, imagine being my age and just now finding you had a child. Wouldn't you want the best for that child?"

"Of course, sir."

"And wouldn't you want to ensure that child was comfortable in her life before you added any possible joy" he paused—"or misery to her life?"

Trevor closed his eyes and battled with himself. He could walk away. Investigating people's private lives was something of a hobby, a chance to earn extra money, and just a little dangerous sometimes too. It was living out a childhood fantasy. Going back to New York and investigating insurance frauds and claims paid the bills. His apartment was nice enough and so was his office. Things were comfortable.

But what if a woman did to him what Mandy Marlow had done to Donald Buchanan? What if he'd fathered a child and wasn't even given the knowledge that he was a father? What if his daughter had been given to her ex-lover to raise?

A sharp disgust began to brew in Trevor when he thought about the injustice that Mandy Marlow had done to Donald Buchanan. What if Hope wasn't happy in her life and Mandy had thrust her into a family that took her, but didn't love her?

Wouldn't it be his job to find out and offer Hope an alternative? What if she didn't like the Kendals at all? What if she'd always wished to be someone else? He could offer her something no one else could—the truth.

He'd have to accept Donald's offer, and of course, the fees that went along with that, and get to know Hope Kendal a little better before he could decide which path he should take in helping her.

"It shouldn't be a problem to get to know her better."

"Thank you for all that you're doing." Donald took a deep breath. "Mr. Jacobs, if I may ask, what is the first name of my daughter?"

Trevor contemplated what he was asking and realized that Donald hadn't asked for too much information. He too was keeping to the contract of what he'd asked Trevor to do. "Her name is Hope."

"Hope." Donald sighed. "Thank you."

The line went dead.

Trevor watched as the lights began to turn off in the apartment in the reverse order from how she'd turned them on. He also realized he'd stayed parked outside her apartment longer than he'd meant to. Donald Buchanan had asked him to find out about her family, he reminded himself. He ensured himself that was what he was doing. He'd follow her and see where she went. Maybe she'd lead him to her family.

He was just doing his job.

Then he saw her on her front stoop. She wore a short white dress. Her hair fell down her back in lazy curls. She locked the door to her apartment and hurried toward her car.

The thudding of his heart was a surprise. The sweating of his palms and the drying of his mouth combined into a clash of discomfort. He watched her now without the interest of a private investigator, but that of a protector. But whom was he protecting her from? He'd just moved into a very strange role of stalker, though the feelings inside of him were much different.

He needed to meet her again, and this time, get to know her—and stop following her like a voyeur. He drove away in the opposite direction, disgusted with himself for having sat on her street. He needed to justify himself again with a long hot shower and an ice-cold beer before he decided how he was going to approach Hope Kendal.

Hope climbed into her car as quickly as she could and locked the door. The tingling in her hand had returned when she'd locked the door to her apartment. She looked around. She could feel him.

She blew out a ragged breath as she started the car and turned onto the street. He was just in her mind, that was all. By tomorrow, she would have forgotten all about him.

She pulled up in front of the house where her great-grandmother and mother had grown up. Now her sister and her family lived in the house that almost a century earlier had been a boardinghouse.

Hope's nieces ran through the yard as she climbed out of her car.

"Auntie Hope!" Becky jumped into her arms. "You're going to let me help you open the book Mommy bought you, aren't you?"

"Becky!" Julie's eyes were wide as she stared in disbelief at her little sister. At eight she'd learned the fine art of keeping a secret. "Mom is going to kill you for telling her."

"I'm sure you're mother won't kill her. But I won't tell her I know." Hope set Becky on the ground.

"Tell me you know what?"

Hope looked up to see her sister standing in the doorway with her arms crossed over her chest.

"That Becky told Auntie Hope what her present was," Julie told her mother, her voice filled with disgust.

Hope watched as a smile slid across her sister's lips and a laugh then escaped her throat.

Julie stomped her feet up the front steps to the house.

"Why are you laughing? Isn't she in trouble?"

Hope cocked an eyebrow at her sister. "I'm not getting a book, am I?"

Carissa stepped back so Hope and Becky could enter the house. "I knew someone would spill the beans. I guess you'll all be surprised, won't you?"

"Mom, that's not fair!" Becky protested.

"Well, I guess I knew you couldn't keep a secret," Carissa said as she patted her daughter on the bottom and sent her off laughing. "Mom, Dad, and Thomas are in the kitchen." She laced her arm with Hope's.

"You'll be glad to know I was working too hard to remember to buy treats."

"Glad to hear it. But you were working on your birthday?"

"Painting."

"Ah, you got inspired today?"

Hope stopped.

"I met a man today," she said and noticed that Carissa's eyes widened. "Right after you left, he walked by searching for his aunt's grave."

"Was he cute?"

Hope laughed. "Oh my God! He was amazing."

"You were painting him?"

"His face won't leave my mind. He shook my hand and there was such a shock that passed through us, I can still feel it." She clasped her hands together.

"And if I know you, you think that was a sign?" Carissa was studying her and Hope smiled at her sister.

"It was nice, that's all." She took her sister's arm again and they headed to the kitchen.

The aromas of Thomas's signature spaghetti sauce filled the house and had Hope's stomach growling. It was only then she realized she hadn't eaten anything since her bagel that morning before heading to the cemetery. Her mind had been too occupied to think of food.

Her father was the first to cross to her.

"Happy birthday, sweetheart." He kissed her on the cheek a smiled down at her.

David Kendal, father of the year, every year, in her book. She knew she'd only be happy when she found a man like her father.

He'd been a pilot until up until the beginning of the year when he'd retired. Hope wasn't sure when he'd had time to work. He and her mother had been going nonstop since they'd cleaned up the retirement party.

They had traveled Europe and spent a month in Australia. They spent time in Italy with her former boss Pablo DiAngelo and his partner Pierre before returning home and planting the biggest garden in the city and taken on the role of babysitter for Carissa's children. Happiness was truly theirs.

He wore his sixty-three years handsomely. His hair was pure silver, but as he always said, "It let go of the color but at least it didn't let go."

Well-deserved lines peeked from the corners of his eyes. There had been a lot of world seen through them.

"Thank you, Daddy." She fell into his shoulder as he wrapped an arm around her.

"Stop hogging her." Sophia Kendal wiped her hands on a towel and crossed the kitchen to hug her. "Happy birthday, darling."

Her mother kissed her on the cheek and beamed at her. Hope couldn't imagine that a child born into a family could be more loved than she was. Luck had been on her side when her birth mother had given her to them. They hadn't chosen her, but they had taken her, and loved her.

"There's my girl!" Thomas put down his spoon and turned from the stove to envelop Hope in another hug. "I got your favorite almost finished. Why don't you get the kids to wash up and sit down?"

"I can do that much." Hope smiled at her brother-in-law. Carissa was a lucky woman. Sophia had set her sister and Thomas up to fall in love, just as her grandma Katie had done for Sophia and David years ago. Matchmaking. It seemed to be a family trait that lead to happiness. Hope could only assume they hadn't found the right man yet, or she'd have fallen willing victim to their skills as well.

As they gathered around the table Hope sat, as she often did, in awe of the commotion that ensued. Over the years, as each member of the family was added, she'd come accustomed to the changes at the table. Certain people sat in certain chairs. Some would eat their peas. Others would tuck them under other items on their plate to hide them.

Her sister never actually sat down, and her meal wasn't touched until her four beautiful children bounded from the table to find something better to do.

Thomas could carry on a conversation with every person at the table simultaneously. Her mother had taken on her great-grandmother's art of gossip. Never did Sophia say a harsh word though. She enjoyed sharing the happenings of those she knew.

Her father, as usual, was more reserved. He kept his words, she always mused, until he was ready to use them, and then he'd use them all.

Dinnertime at Carissa's was noisy, and messy, and always the one thing Hope looked forward to being a part of.

Thomas left the table and returned a moment later with a bottle of champagne. "I have something special for tonight. In honor of the birthday girl."

Hope smiled wide. "Oh, you shouldn't have."

"Can I have some?" Becky asked.

"You can have a little taste," Thomas promised, though Hope knew he wouldn't have his own. He didn't drink. She'd never seen him drink. She'd been told that he drank plenty once. It had been enough to nearly kill him.

Thomas opened the bottle and sniffed it.

"I don't think you'll like it, Becky."

"Oh, it's an adult thing," she said with her face already scrunched up. Hope's heart went out to her. She'd been that girl not so long ago. With Carissa being seventeen years older than she was, she'd shared the table with adults her entire life and wanted to always be just like them.

Hope wrapped her arm around her niece's shoulders.

"Well, if you'd rather not have the bubbly stuff, then I think you should have a bigger piece of cake."

"Really, Auntie Hope? I can have a bigger piece of cake?"

"That is, if there *is* cake." She looked around at the others at the table.

Sophia crossed her arms over her chest and shot her chin up. "Have I ever missed baking you a birthday cake?"

"Not once." Hope reached across the table and placed her hand on her mother's.

Sophia Kendal, what an amazing woman. What woman took on the responsibility of another person's child and loved her like Sophia had loved her?

Hope sat back and sipped her champagne, listening to the chaos, and thinking. She'd battled with the thought for years. Had Mandy had a change of heart and given her to David because she actually loved her? Or was she hoping to punish him by dumping a baby on him and then dying? They'd all told her what he was willing to sacrifice to keep her, and she wasn't even his blood. He could have lost

Sophia altogether, but he wanted to give Hope a home and he wanted her with her sister. Not a day had gone by in her life that she hadn't thanked God that David had decided to keep her and that Sophia had fallen in love with her.

Sophia carried the cake from the kitchen and set it in front of Hope. Precisely placed on the cake were twenty-three candles.

Becky snuggled in next to her aunt. "I counted them and put them on the cake."

"I think you put too many."

"Nope. Mama said to put two whole boxes on and then take one off."

"Well now that is one smart mama." Hope touched her head to her niece's as she watched Thomas light the candles on her cake.

This family, her real family, was all the family she would ever need.

Meet the Author

Bernadette Marie has been an avid writer since the early age of 13, when she'd fill notebook after notebook with stories that she'd share with her friends. Her journey into novel writing started the summer before eighth grade when her father gave her an old typewriter. At all times of the day and night you would find her on the back porch penning her first work, which she would continue to write for the next 22 years.

In 2007—after marriage, filling her chronic entrepreneurial needs, and having five children—Bernadette began to write seriously with the goal of being published. That year she wrote 12 books. In 2009 she was contracted for her first trilogy and the published author was born. In 2011 she (being the entrepreneur that she is) opened her own publishing house, 5 Prince Publishing, and has released her own contemporary titles. She also quickly began the process of taking on other authors in other genres.

In 2012 Bernadette Marie began to find herself on the bestsellers lists of iTunes, Amazon, and Barnes and Noble to name a few. Her office wall is lined with colorful PostIt notes with the titles of books she will be releasing in the very near future, with hope that they too will grace the bestsellers lists.

Bernadette spends most of her free time driving her kids to their many events—usually hockey. She is also an accomplished martial artist with a second degree black belt in Tang Soo Do. An avid reader, she enjoys contemporary romances with humor and happily ever afters.

Other titles published by
www.5princebooks.com

Split Decisions *Carmen DeSousa*
Matchmakers *Bernadette Marie*
Rocky Road *Susan Lohrer*
Stutter Creek *Ann Swann*
The Perfect Crime *P. Hindley, S. Goodsell*
Lost and Found *Bernadette Marie*
A Heart at Home *Sara Barnard*
Soul Connection *Doug Simpson*
Bridge Over the Atlantic *Lisa Hobman*
An Unexpected Admirer *Bernadette Marie*
The Italian Job *Phyllis Humphrey*
Jaded *M.J. Kane*
Shades of Darkness *Melynda Price*
Heart Like an Ocean *Christine Steendam*
The Depot *Carmen DeSousa*
Crisis of Identity *Denise Moncrief*
A Heart Broken *Sara Barnard*
Soul Mind *Doug Simpson*
Chunky Sugars *Sara Barnard*
When Noonday Ends *Carmen DeSousa*
Fatal Jealousy *Christina OW*
Center Stage *Bernadette Marie*
Chris Mouse and the Promise *Tina Adams*
Soul Rescue *Doug Simpson*
The Pit Stop *Carmen DeSousa*
Soul Awakening *Doug Simpson*
First Kiss *Bernadette Marie*
A Heart not Easily Broken *MJ Kane*
Entangled Dreams *Carmen DeSousa*
All For Love *Ann Swann*
Opposite Attraction *Bernadette Marie*